SHEEPDOG IN THE SNOW

"Poor thing!" Mandy gasped. The dog came alongside, head down, trying to creep quietly by. But her injured paw hit against a small rock at the roadside. She yelped and staggered sideways toward them. Mandy and James ran forward to help.

The dog whined, her sides heaved, and she fell at their feet. Gently Mandy put out a hand to stroke her head. The deep brown eyes stared back.

"There, girl, there." Mandy felt like crying for the wounded, starved animal. She looked up at James with tears in her eyes. "We have to get her back to Welford!" she whispered. "Let's get her to Animal Ark."

Read all the Animal Ark books!

by Ben M. Baglio

ANIMAL ARK®

Sheepdog in the Snow

Ben M. Baglio

Illustrations by Shelagh McNicholas

AN
APPLE
PAPERBACK

SCHOLASTIC INC.

New York   Toronto   London   Auckland   Sydney
Mexico City   New Delhi   Hong Kong   Buenos Aires

To the real Tess

Special thanks to Jenny Ol
C.J. Hall, B.Vet.Med., M.R
the veterinary material c

ISBN 0-590-18757-0

Copyright © 1995 by Ben M. Baglio.
Illustrations copyright © 1995 by Shelagh McNicholas.

All rights reserved. Published by Scholastic Inc., 557 Broadway, New York, NY 10012,
by arrangement with Working Partners Limited. ANIMAL ARK is a trademark of
Working Partners Limited. SCHOLASTIC, APPLE PAPERBACKS, and associated
logos are trademarks and/or registered trademarks of Scholastic Inc.

22 21 20 19   5 6 7 8 9/0

Printed in the U.S.A.   40

One

Christmas was coming. Mandy Hope's school had been let out for the holidays. Brightly wrapped presents were stacked under the tree in the cozy kitchen at Animal Ark, and Mandy and her friend James Hunter were hunched over the table surrounded by invitation cards.

"Let's make a list," James suggested. He chewed the end of his pen. "In alphabetical order."

"What kind of list?" Mandy pushed her blond hair behind her ears and scribbled away. She was making out an invitation to Grandma and Grandpa Hope, and Smoky the cat. Each card was hand-designed by James and Mandy. They'd cut out squares of bright yellow

1

poster board, drawn the black outline of a Christmas tree on each one, and written the words "PARTY TIME" across the top.

"A list of guests." James liked to be organized. He didn't want to leave anyone out. He thought Mandy was rushing into things too quickly. "Should we put pets or people first?"

"Pets," came the prompt reply. Mandy filled out her grandparents' card. "A Christmas Eve Party!" it read. "Pets, bring your owners to Welford Village Hall on Saturday, December 24, at 7:30 P.M. Music and Food!" It was signed with a miniature cat's paw print, from a stencil that James had made.

"Okay." James began his list. "Barney and Button . . . Blackie . . . Dorian . . . Eric . . . Houdini. . . ." He ran through the names of some of the pets they'd helped in the past. "Rosa won't be able to come because she's hibernating . . . but Sammy probably will, because squirrels only semihibernate, and —"

"Hang on a second; you left out Ruby and Prince." Mandy remembered the piglet and the pony as she tucked the invitation into an envelope.

"Hmm . . . Can we get a pony into the village hall?" James wondered.

Mandy thought carefully. "I suppose Susan could bring him and stay outside with him. Prince could stick his head through an open window and enjoy things from there."

"And what about pigs?"

She imagined friendly, adventurous Ruby trotting in and out of the trestle tables, rooting for food. She nodded. "Pigs are fine. We want everyone to come, remember. It's going to be the biggest, best Christmas party for pets anyone's ever seen!"

Mandy's blue eyes shone. Animals were the love of her life, and the idea of giving them a Christmas treat, where all the past patients of Animal Ark could get together with pets that Mandy and James had helped to rescue, and farm animals they'd managed to save, promised to make this a Christmas to remember.

She imagined everyone gathered there — cats and dogs, rabbits, hamsters, sheep, and pigs. She wanted to invite Ernie Bell and his squirrel, Sammy; Lydia Fawcett and her wonderful escaping goat, Houdini. She even wanted Pandora the Pekingese and Toby the mongrel, though this would mean having to invite their fussy owner, Mrs. Ponsonby. "I wonder if Pandora will come all dressed up?" Mandy smiled.

"No, but I bet Mrs. Ponsonby will." James pushed his glasses farther up his nose. He slotted Pandora's name into the list. "Hey, let's have a competition for the best party hat!" he suggested.

"And carols. And a Christmas procession down the village street." Mandy could picture the magic scene. For a few moments she stopped to daydream. She'd take along Mopsy, the tamest of her three rabbits, warmly zipped up inside the front of her jacket. They would have to make up a menu of food, from lettuce leaves for Mopsy to oats for Susan Collins's pony. It would be snowing outside, and they would carry candles down the street. They would crowd into the village hall, singing carols. Then the pets would be let loose on the party food. . . .

"Mandy?" James broke in.

"Hmm?"

"I said, do you want to invite Imogen with Button and Barney, or John Hardy?"

"Both," Mandy beamed. She was feeling generous. "You know, Imogen Parker Smythe isn't nearly so spoiled now that she has the two rabbits to look after. In fact, I'd even say she was quite nice!"

"And what about Claire?" James remembered his little, dark-haired next-door neighbor. She ran a hedgehog sanctuary in her garden. "Rosa, Guy, and everyone will be fast asleep for the winter in their nest-boxes."

Mandy's brow wrinkled. "Yes, we can't wake them up specially, just to come to a party. Claire will have to come by herself." She began to make out a fresh invitation. It was only five days until Christmas Eve, and they had lots to do.

In the background they could hear Adam Hope, Mandy's dad, puttering around the house. He went up and downstairs, in and out of the living room, humming and singing to himself. Then he put his bearded face around the kitchen door.

> *Christmas is coming,*
> *The goose is getting fat . . .*

he sang;

> *Please put a penny*
> *In the old man's hat.*
> *If you haven't got a penny,*
> *A halfpenny will do.*
> *If you haven't got a halfpenny,*
> *A farthing will do.*
> *If you haven't got a farthing . . .*

"*God bless you!*" Mandy and James chimed in, their faces wreathed in smiles.

"Busy?" Dr. Adam asked. He picked up an invitation card. "Good idea," he nodded. "Yes. Pets at a party, very good. A get-together, hmm. . . ." He wandered off again, grabbing his white coat from the back of a chair. Then he headed off to the Animal Ark office in the modern extension at the back of their old stone cottage. They heard him "pom-pom-pom"ing on an imaginary trombone as he went.

Mandy grinned at James. She loved her absent-minded, easygoing dad, and she thought his job as a vet in Animal Ark was the best there was. And when she grew up, she wanted to be a vet herself.

"What about Simon and Jean?" James thought of the veterinary assistant and receptionist. "They don't have anyone to bring. Pets, I mean."

"They can come anyway." Mandy watched James add them to the list. She jumped up from the table, uncurling her fingers and stretching her arms. "I have writer's cramp," she said. "How about going to ask Simon and Jean right now?"

James didn't need a second prompting. He liked the office, its reception area crowded during business hours with animal patients — hairy and sleek, big and tiny, noisy and silent. He was out of his seat and through the door before Mandy had finished stretching. He headed for the extension and its meowing, shuffling, snuffling patients.

James and Mandy rushed in to say hello to the people and pets they knew from the village and farms surrounding Welford. They noticed Jack Spiller, with his daughter, Jenny, and their old sheepdog. They worked on a small farm out of town. The dog had scratched her eye and it was infected, Jack said. He kept a close watch on Sam Western, who was also in the reception area with his new dog — a large German shepherd, mostly black, with a pale brown face and chest. He was a fine animal, but he seemed edgy. Sam Western didn't keep his dogs up at Upper Welford Hall as pets, but as guard dogs to chase off trespassers. Mandy bent to talk gently to the nervous animal. "What's his name?" she asked Mr. Western.

"Major." The reply was brisk. Mr. Western looked impatiently at his watch. "How much longer?" he asked Jean Knox.

The gray-haired receptionist checked the appointment book. "You're next, Mr. Western. It shouldn't be long now."

"They're running five minutes late in there," he complained. Sam Western was a busy and important man, and he liked everyone to know it.

Mandy smiled and stroked Major; then she and James approached the reception desk.

"What are you doing this Saturday, Jean?" Mandy leaned both elbows on the counter.

"Let's see, Saturday? Why, that's Christmas Eve, isn't

it?" Jean counted out the days on her fingers. "As a matter of fact, I don't have anything planned." She peered at them over her glasses.

"Would you like to come to a party at the village hall?" James asked. "It's for everyone from Animal Ark and their owners."

Jean took off her glasses and put her head to one side. "Shouldn't that be 'everyone and their *pets*'?"

"No, it's a *pets'* party," Mandy insisted. "But there'll be food and drink for people, too." She felt grateful that her mom and Mrs. Hunter, James's mom, had both agreed to contribute toward the cost. "We'd like everyone to come."

"Well, I suppose I could fit in making my mince pies earlier in the day. And I go to midnight mass, but that's much later, of course. Yes, I'd be delighted, thank you!" She beamed at them and began searching the counter. "Let me write that down!"

"Here's a pen." James handed her one. "It begins at seven-thirty."

Jean took the pen and looked helplessly for a spare scrap of paper.

"Here!" Mandy took one from her pocket. "And your glasses are around your neck." She was used to helping their receptionist find the things she'd lost.

Jean smiled again as she fixed them on her nose. "Ah, thank you, Mandy dear." She looked across the room as the door to the exam room opened. Walter Pickard emerged with his elderly cat, Tom. "Mr. Western, you can take Major in now."

Mandy went up to her old friend Walter, who lived in the row of small cottages beside the Fox and Goose tavern. "What's Tom been up to?" She tickled the cat's chin. "His ear's kind of a mess, isn't it?"

"He's been in a fight," the old man grumbled. "You'd think he'd know better."

Burly Tom looked as if he couldn't care less. Bitten ear or not, the next chance he got, he'd be tussling again. He purred proudly as Mandy inspected his chewed ear.

They stood to one side as Mr. Western pushed past toward the treatment room. He held Major on a short leash, but the dog managed to lift his head and growl at old Tom.

Simon stood at the door, waiting. When he spotted Mandy, he spoke rapidly. "Grab a white coat and give me a hand in here, would you? We're running behind." He smiled at Mr. Western and escorted him into the small, clean white room.

"Is that okay?" Mandy checked with James.

He nodded. "I'll go and do some more invitations. We'd better get up to High Cross later today to call on Lydia and on the Parker Smythes."

Mandy agreed. "I won't be long," she promised.

Inside the treatment room, Simon had already lifted the big German shepherd dog onto the table. Mr. Western stood against the wall. The dog's ears were laid flat, its teeth bared. But Simon dealt with him expertly and calmly, stroking his long back and encouraging him to stand still. "This is a magnificent animal you have here, Mr. Western," he said. "Where did you get him?"

"From a house in York. Small yard. Hopeless." Mr. Western didn't smile. He used words sparingly, as if they cost money.

"No good at all for a guy this size," Simon agreed. "You need plenty of space to run around in, don't you, boy?" He inspected the dog's ears and gently eased open his jaw. "He hasn't been ill-treated, at least."

Mr. Western grunted. "He just needs his injections. I don't want him keeling over on me, not after what I've just paid for him. And I don't want him infecting the other two dogs either."

Mandy frowned and went to a drawer to get rubber gloves and a syringe pack for Simon, while he took the drugs from a high, locked cupboard. Mr. Western owned a large estate nearby. He was a dairy farmer, using modern methods, but, strangely, he didn't seem to like animals. He was stocky and bad-tempered, and ran his place strictly. Mandy imagined a stern, open-air life for Major from now on, after his cooped-up existence in the city.

Simon spoke soothingly to the dog while Mandy stood at his head, holding his collar firmly. He jerked as Simon gave the injection, and his back legs shifted, but he gave no other sign. "That's it; good boy," Simon said. Mandy let him jump easily to the floor.

Quickly Mr. Western hooked the dog's leash back on. "That's it, you're finished?" he asked. Simon nodded. With a curt "thank-you," the farmer left the room. "Put this down on my account," he told Jean. Soon the outer doors were swinging behind him and his new guard dog.

"Simon!" Mandy found time for a quiet word before the next patient came in. She'd disposed of the gloves and syringe in a special sealed bin. "Are you doing anything on Christmas Eve?" She prayed he could come to their party. He could bring his music collection and be the disc jockey.

"Not much so far." When he heard Mandy's offer, he said he'd love to come.

She smiled. *So far, so good,* she thought.

Then it was time to get busy again, tending to a wounded rabbit's paw, inoculating another dog, binding up a kitten's sprained back leg.

Time flew. Before Mandy knew it, morning office hours were over and she was free to go back to James and the party preparations.

Two

By midday Mandy and James had gathered their pile of carefully addressed envelopes, put them into their coat pockets, and set off on their bikes for High Cross. It was a clear, sunny Monday as they biked down the driveway from Animal Ark, under the wooden sign swinging in the cold wind. As far as the eye could see, down the valley to the riverside, and up the steep, soaring hillsides to the Beacon and High Cross Farm, the air was crisp and bright. The trees stood gray and bare. The hills were a range of dull browns and sharp greens.

Mandy's breath clouded the freezing air. She pedaled hard to get warm. Soon she and James were riding through the village, up the main street, past the Fox and Goose, the church and the village hall, where their great event was to take place.

Their first stop was Bleakfell Hall, Mrs. Ponsonby's grand house just outside the village. "Might as well get this over with," Mandy sighed, knowing that Mrs. Ponsonby would go on and on about poor Pandora's latest mystery ailment. Even though Pandora was perfectly healthy, Mrs. Ponsonby seemed to bring the Pekingese to Animal Ark virtually every week. Mandy swung open the gate, and together she and James pedaled up the driveway.

The front door opened, and Pandora and Toby came flying out of the house to greet them, yapping and jumping up in pleasure.

"Down, Toby, down!" Mrs. Ponsonby scolded. She followed them out, wearing a pink flowered apron over her royal blue dress. Her round, plump face was set off by pink winged glasses with a sparkling rhinestone decoration. She ignored the fact that her beloved Pandora was gnawing at James's trouser leg, and bore down instead on poor Toby. "Bad boy! Down!"

Mandy smiled at the friendly mongrel and told him to sit. Toby obliged. His tail wagged to and fro against the gravel driveway. Mandy put down her bike, pulled out Mrs. Ponsonby's invitation, and handed it to her.

"What's this?" she exclaimed. She tore open the envelope in great excitement. "Oh, a party!" she read. Then her face changed. She frowned. "What's this? A party for pets? Oh, no; I don't think so, my dear." She shook her head.

"Why not?" Mandy looked in dismay at Pandora and Toby.

Mrs. Ponsonby creaked forward to scoop up a dog under each arm. "Pandora's not very strong, you see. A party would be too much for her. I'm afraid I will have to say no."

Pandora whined and wheezed.

"What about Toby?" James stood astride his bike, inspecting the small holes in the leg of his jeans.

"Toby can't go without his best friend, Pandora, can you, Toby-Woby?" Mrs. Ponsonby made squeaking noises with her lips. "That wouldn't be fair on Pandy-Wandy, now would it?" She glanced up at Mandy. "I'm afraid we shall have to decline your kind offer."

Mandy swallowed hard. It was a shame that the two pets would miss out. She knew for a fact that Pandora was as tough as the next dog; it was only Mrs. Ponsonby's fussy nature that made her see death and disaster around every corner. "I'm sorry you can't come." She picked up her bike and leaned forward to give the dogs a pat.

For a moment, Mrs. Ponsonby seemed to be about to change her mind. "I suppose your mother and father will be there to supervise?" She tried to sound casual. "And your grandparents?"

Mandy nodded. "I've already asked Grandma unofficially. She's promised to help with the food."

This seemed unwelcome news to Mrs. Ponsonby. She stepped back and sniffed. "Really? Has Dorothy asked for permission?"

Mandy remembered, too late, that bossy Mrs. Ponsonby and Grandma rarely saw eye to eye. They both loved to organize, but neither liked to take orders from the other. "What for?" she asked.

"To take food into the village hall. You must ask the pastor's permission, you know. It's a church hall, after all. In fact, Reverend Hadcroft is rather particular about it. He doesn't like a mess."

"Oh. I'll check," Mandy said flatly. She put it at the top of her list of things to do. "Let's go and ask Grandma about it," she said to James with a worried look. It was too late to change the party venue now, with Christmas Eve only five days away and the invitations already written out. . . .

"Take no notice of Mrs. Ponsonby," said Grandma.

Mandy and James had biked right over to Lilac Cottage. "She's only trying to throw a monkey wrench in the works." Her eyes sparkled and she spoke firmly. "It's because you asked *me* to help with the food, you see. Amelia Ponsonby can't bear anyone else to do the organizing. Now, if you'd asked *her*, my dear, I'm sure that she would have turned around and decided that Pandora was as fit as a fiddle after all, and she'd be down at the village hall right this minute, buttering mountains of sliced bread for sandwiches."

Mandy grinned with relief.

"No, don't worry. Reverend Hadcroft won't mind in the least little bit. And life will be quieter without Mrs. Ponsonby breathing down our necks!"

"It's too bad about Toby and Pandora, though," James said wistfully as they rode up the hill toward High Cross at last. "And all because Mrs. Ponsonby doesn't get to make the sandwiches."

They had to stop talking to concentrate on the steep climb. It made them hot and breathless, even on this crisp winter's day. When they reached the top and stopped beside some big iron gates, they saw the Parker Smythe mansion locked up, with no cars in the driveway. James went to slip Imogen's invitation into the mailbox. Then they were on their way again, past Sam Western's barking dogs on the grounds of his huge farm, on to the small stone farmhouse at the end of the path. It stood almost in the shadow of the ancient Celtic monument — Lydia Fawcett's goat farm, High Cross.

As she heard them approach, gentle, shy Lydia came out of the barn. She was dressed in her old brown work coat and boots. She smiled as she strode to meet them, leading high-stepping Houdini. The black-and-white goat had a wicked light in his eye and snickered a greeting. Mandy ran up and gave him a hug. "How would you like to come to a Christmas party, Houdini?" she asked.

"And you, too, Lydia." James handed her the invitation.

Lydia hemmed and hawed. She wasn't a party sort of person. She had her goats to look after. She didn't get down to the village much during these dark evenings.

"But it's Christmas Eve!" Mandy protested. She knew that Lydia didn't drive a car. "Listen, I'm sure I can get my dad to drive up in the jeep and get you and Houdini, and bring you safely back again. He wouldn't mind!"

Lydia blushed, and though she said she wouldn't dream of putting Dr. Adam out in that way, she gradually gave way to her friends' pleas. "Ernie will be there with Sammy," James promised. "You'll know tons of people. Please come, Lydia!"

Houdini nodded his head impatiently. They all laughed at him. "Very well," Lydia said at last. "Just so you know, I don't have any pretty party dresses."

"Come as you are," Mandy smiled. "Just as long as you come!"

They waved and rode off down the path, pleased with their success at persuading their shy friend and their favorite goat.

"Where to next?" James asked. They sped along the high hill road. The village nestled in the valley bottom. They could see for miles.

"Ernie and Sammy's?" Mandy suggested. "Since we've already told Lydia they'll be there!" It was a white lie, and all in a good cause.

James agreed. Ernie Bell had built the strong fences that kept Lydia's goats safely penned in. The two were good company for each other; Ernie was always less grumpy when Lydia was around, and Lydia was less shy. "Let's hope he says yes," he said. Besides, Sammy the squirrel was one of his favorite pets.

But they'd only pedaled a few more yards before a movement on the winding road ahead caught Mandy's eye. She braked and waited for the shape to reappear out of a hollow. It was heading slowly in their direction.

"What's wrong?" James slowed down beside her.

"I think there's an animal on the road." Mandy glanced around for traffic danger, but the exposed hill road was deserted. "There it is again, look!" She pointed. A black creature came up the hill.

"It's a dog." James saw it, too. "I think it's limping."

Quickly Mandy lay down her bike against the grass at the road's edge. "Don't scare it. Let's wait here." What was a dog doing in the middle of nowhere on a cold, raw day like this?

James and Mandy stood waiting for the dog to approach. It came with a halting step, its left front paw so sore that it could scarcely touch the ground.

"It looks like some kind of sheepdog," James whispered. "Do you think it's lost?"

Mandy shook her head. "I don't know. It's not from around here, though. At least, I don't recognize it."

The dog limped along. Its head hung low, its tongue lolled, its tail brushed the ground. The wind blew in its face as it mounted the hill, slowing it almost to a standstill.

"Poor thing!" Mandy's heart went out at once to the suffering creature. She saw it was female. "Look how thin she is!" She squatted down and called to the dog. "Here, girl, here!"

The dog lifted her dull head and caught sight of them at last. She halted, too weary to avoid them by heading off across the grass and over the low stone wall into the field beyond. She whined and hung her head.

"She must be starving!" James knelt down at Mandy's

side. "Here, girl. Look, she's not wearing a collar or a name tag. Who knows how far she's walked?"

Mandy sighed. "Who's left her here?" Again she scanned the countryside, but there was no sign of an owner, either in a car or on foot.

Eventually the dog seemed strong enough to resume her limping progress. She moved forward. From close up, they could see that her black coat was matted and the underside of her long tail was tangled with mud and thorns. Her front paws, speckled gray and white, were a dull, muddy brown. Worst of all, her thin sides heaved with the effort of hauling herself up the long hill. Through her coat they could see the shape of her rib cage and the lean, starved haunches.

"Poor thing!" Mandy gasped again. The dog came alongside, head down, trying to creep quietly by. But her injured paw hit against a small rock at the roadside. She yelped and staggered sideways toward them. Mandy and James ran forward to help.

The dog whined, her sides heaved, and she fell at their feet. She lay on her side, eyes and mouth open, tongue lolling. Gently Mandy put out a hand to stroke her head. The deep brown eyes stared back.

"There, girl, there." Mandy felt like crying for the wounded, starved animal. She looked up at James with tears in her eyes. "We have to get her back to Welford!" she whispered. "Let's get her to Animal Ark."

"She's nearly dead, poor thing!" James warned Mandy to be gentle.

The dog lay in the road. She made one sad attempt to wag her tail in greeting, as if she knew that these were her rescuers. She gave herself up to James and Mandy's care, closed her eyes, and slipped gently into unconsciousness.

Three

Quickly Mandy unzipped her warm woolen jacket and wrapped the dog inside it. "I'll leave my bike here," she told James. "Can you go ahead and tell Mom and Dad what's happening?" Ever so gently, she edged her arms under the limp body and lifted it from the cold ground.

"Are you sure you can carry her?" James stood astride his bike, his face pale and worried.

She nodded. "I'll manage. Get someone to bring the car out. Hurry, please!" Steadying herself, she began to carry the dog down the hill.

James set off, crouched over his handlebars, speeding into the dip, pedaling for all he was worth up the other side. He was soon out of sight.

Mandy trudged on. The dog didn't weigh much, even wrapped inside Mandy's coat. She was mostly skin and bone, but she heaved a sigh and her eyelids fluttered. Mandy spoke gently to her as she walked. "There, girl, there. We'll soon have you back safe and sound." Inside her head, another voice whispered, *Let's hope we're not too late!*

Several minutes passed. Still Mandy walked on toward Welford. Only one car passed her, traveling in the other direction. Two curious faces looked out, but the car roared by.

Mandy's arms began to ache. The dog was a dead weight cradled against her chest.

At last she caught sight of the Animal Ark jeep speeding along the road toward her, her mom at the wheel. As the car pulled up, Mandy gave a gasp of relief. "Oh, Mom, thank heavens!"

Emily Hope and James leaped out. Dr. Emily hurried across and took a quick glance at the unconscious sheepdog. She ran back for her bag. "Bring her over here as quickly as you can," she told Mandy, flinging open the back door. "Lay her down. That's right. Now stand back and let me take a good look."

Mandy put the poor creature into the back of the car. She straightened up and peered anxiously over her mother's shoulder, knowing that if anyone could save the dog, Emily Hope could.

"She's badly dehydrated," Dr. Emily said after pinching the dog's skin. "Now, James, pass me that glucose solution. That's the one." She made sure the dog stayed warmly wrapped inside the jacket, then she lifted her head and offered a few drops of the sweet liquid by mouth, through a syringe feed. They saw the dog's throat constrict and swallow. Her pink tongue passed across her lips. Dr. Emily gave her a few drops more.

Soon her eyes opened and she was licking and swallowing greedily.

Mandy looked across at James. She sighed. Dr. Emily stroked the dog's throat to help her swallow. They saw the tip of her tail wag free of her makeshift blanket. "Is she going to make it?" Mandy asked.

Her mom stood up. "Let's hope so, thanks to you two!" She told them to hop into the car. "She was pretty far gone. Mandy, you sit here. Let the dog rest her head against your knees. Talk quietly to her and keep her calm while I drive back home."

Quickly Mandy climbed in and followed instructions.

James stood by the jeep, checking that Mandy and the dog were safely inside. "I'll go back for your bike and ride down," he told her as he closed the door.

Mandy and Dr. Emily agreed. Emily Hope backed up into a driveway, turned, and set off, roaring down the hillside. In the back of the car, Mandy softly stroked the dog's dark head, lying in her lap, staring up at her with her big, faithful brown eyes. "Please get better," Mandy whispered. She felt she'd never wanted anything more in her life than for this beautiful, gentle creature to return to health.

* * *

Simon ran out into the office yard as the jeep pulled up. He opened the back door and gathered the patient in his arms. Adam Hope stood waiting at the door.

Stiffly Mandy clambered out, following Simon and her mother. "I don't think there are any broken bones, just cuts and sores. She's badly dehydrated," Dr. Emily reported. "We need to remove something sharp from her left front pad and treat the infected area. Otherwise, it's a case of warmth, lots of liquid, and rest." She hurried into the treatment room.

Simon laid the dog on a treatment table, leaving the warm cover over her. She raised her head.

Mandy's father took a look. He felt gently with his fingertips, checking joints, listening for the heartbeat through his stethoscope. He looked up at Mandy. "She doesn't seem too bad," he said. "Very thin, though. It's a disgrace!" His voice was low and intense. "How can people let an animal get into this condition?"

Emily Hope put on some rubber gloves and took a pair of small tweezers from the sterile unit. She crouched down, talking gently to the dog as she took hold of the injured paw, swabbed the affected area, and deftly pulled a sharp object from the wound. She held it up to the light. "A splinter of glass," she reported.

The dog whined and tried to rise.

"Steady," Simon said. He stroked her neck.

"Look, she wants to get up!" Mandy said. The dog had struggled free of the jacket.

Adam Hope nodded. "Let her try. Let's see if she can make it. She looks very determined."

Simon eased the jacket away completely. They could all clearly see her starved, shaking body. Slowly she bent her back legs under her and eased herself up at the front. She straightened the back legs until at last she struggled up onto all fours.

Mandy came forward with a bowl of clean drinking water. She put it down within easy reach. Soon the dog lapped noisily, her flanks heaving, her tail wagging low and slow as she drank.

Dr. Adam smiled. "She's tough," he said admiringly. "I wonder where she came from."

"Is she lost?" Dr. Emily wondered. Satisfied with the treatment she began to clear away.

Simon folded his arms and watched the dog enjoy her drink. "This type of dog doesn't usually get lost. Their sense of direction is too good. She's more likely to have been abandoned, I'd say."

Mandy frowned. "You mean someone just dumped her?" She couldn't believe that anyone would do such a thing.

Her dad held up his hand. "Now, we're not sure. There may be a worried owner out there, searching high and low."

They all stood and considered this. "How can we find out?" Mandy noticed the dog wanting to jump down from the table, but she was too weak to attempt it. Checking first with her father, Mandy went to help. She lifted the dog and set her gently down on the floor.

"Hmm . . ." Dr. Adam stroked his beard. "Let me call around. Someone might have heard of a Border collie that's missing."

Mandy knew that her father was in close touch with all the vets in the area. His network of friends and colleagues might well turn up the owner. She nodded. "Do it now, please, Dad!"

He smiled at her earnest expression. "Right away."

"And you could try the SPCA and the Canine Defense League," Emily Hope suggested. At last she found time to take off her own jacket and scarf. Her long, wavy red hair hung free.

"Say it's an emergency," Mandy pleaded. "Say she has no collar, so we don't have a clue where she's from. Someone's probably frantic about her!"

Nodding, Dr. Adam went out into reception.

Dr. Emily came up to Mandy and put an arm around her shoulder. "Don't get your hopes too high," she warned.

"Yes, but . . ." Mandy began to protest.

"Look, maybe there's no frantic owner out there. Maybe the *last* thing that person wants is to get a phone call just before Christmas saying that we've found their dog. As we were saying, the collar's missing. And these sheepdogs are bred and trained to know their way around. They hardly ever get lost." She shook her head. "We'll do our best. But don't expect too much, Mandy. We'll just have to wait and see."

Mandy hung her head. She was glad when, five minutes later, they heard James come running into the office. It broke the anxious ticking of the clock. "The dog's fine," she told him, watching him crouch down and put an arm around her neck.

James stood up straight and gave her a high five.

"Dad's calling around now to see if we can trace where she came from."

They waited all evening for a return call — the news that a sheepdog had been reported missing from a farm on the other side of the county, or that a child in Leeds or York was pining over a missing pet. But the phone didn't ring. Night fell, and Mandy and James made the dog comfortable in a warm bed in a kennel in the residential unit at the back of the office.

Mandy gave her a small amount of ground food. The dog came and nuzzled gratefully against her, then sank into bed. Mandy smiled softly, turned off the light, and left the collie to sleep.

Four

The next morning, Mandy woke and looked out of her bedroom window to see a hard frost covering the ground. She ran downstairs, but before she could ask, her mother shook her head. "No. No news," she said. "But we know one thing for sure; if that poor animal had stayed out last night, there's no way she would have survived! She would have died of hypothermia, and that's a fact!"

Mandy sat down to breakfast, sipping slowly at her orange juice. "But you think she's been abandoned?" she asked.

"It's beginning to look that way."

Mandy shook her head. It was unbelievable; the beautiful dog was unloved, unwanted. And that left them with a problem; who would take her now?

In the middle of this puzzle, Mandy's grandparents stopped by. They were on their way to Walton, the nearest town, and Grandma was armed with a long list of food for the party: dog biscuits, apples, carrots, sugar cubes, and birdseed. Grandpa kept the human list safe in his pocket: rolls, cheese, pigs in blankets, potato chips, chocolate cookies.

They came into the kitchen to see Mandy brooding over her cornflakes. "A penny for your thoughts?" Grandpa said.

Mandy gave a wan smile.

"What's wrong, love?" Grandma came and sat at the table, her voice full of concern. "I can tell the party isn't uppermost in your mind, for a start." She put away the list that she'd intended to discuss with Mandy. "In fact, I can see you're not yourself at all."

Mandy let her empty spoon droop into the bowl. "We rescued a dog yesterday," she explained. "It was starving to death, up in the hills."

Grandma patted her hand. "Well done, dear. But what's the trouble?"

"She's gorgeous, Grandma. Absolutely beautiful. Her face is so trusting. You just have to look into her eyes and you can't help falling in love with her!" To Mandy, this wasn't just any old dog. She felt from the start that she'd rescued someone very special.

Grandma nodded. "So?"

"So how can anyone bear to part with her?" Mandy felt a lump rise in her throat. She was unable to go on.

Grandma got to her feet. "Why don't you show me and Grandpa this wonderful creature?" she suggested with a smile. "I'm sure we'd love to take a look."

Willingly Mandy obliged. She led her grandparents around the side of the house to the unit, through the door and down the row of kennels where the overnight patients stayed. A brown-and-black beagle sat, its head cocked to one side. A King Charles spaniel wagged its tail. At the end of the row, they came to the stray Border collie.

"Well!" Grandpa bent forward and peered through the wire mesh. "She looks happy to see you."

Mandy unbolted the door. The dog was still too weak to jump up, but she wagged her tail. "Come on, girl; let's take you for a little walk."

The dog trotted obediently after her.

"She's limping," Grandma pointed out.

Mandy explained about the splinter of glass. "The foot's already getting better, though."

"She's very thin." Grandpa watched her limp forward from the unit out onto the lawn. She began to sniff happily at a tree trunk, tramping through the frosty grass.

Mandy sighed. "How could anyone do this?"

Grandma and Grandpa stood watching the dog. "Do what, exactly?" Grandpa had his hands in his quilted vest pockets. He blew clouds of steam as he spoke.

"Dump her. Leave her to starve."

Grandma nodded. "It's a shame. Are you sure that's what happened?"

"It looks like it." Mandy had taken her mom's warning to heart. At first she'd been slow to believe that the dog had been abandoned, but why had no one come forward to claim her or put out a message to say that she was missing? How had she lost her collar and name tag unless someone had deliberately taken it off?"

The dog went and sniffed at the hedge bottom, then trotted toward them. She sat by Mandy's side once more.

"Good girl." Mandy bent down to pat her head.

"People do these things," Grandma said quietly. "Especially at Christmas. They go away for the holiday. The dog's a nuisance. They can't afford to put it in a kennel, so they drive into the middle of the countryside and abandon it."

Mandy felt her stomach turn. She bent to put her arms around the dog's neck.

"They should think harder before they get a dog in the first place," Grandpa put in. "But then, people don't. They like the look of them when they're puppies, and they buy them without stopping to consider what's involved in looking after a grown-up dog."

"Especially at this time of year," Grandma reminded them. "Remember. 'A dog is for life, not just for Christmas,'" she quoted the saying. "Not everyone keeps that in mind, I'm afraid."

Mandy looked up at them and sighed.

"I expect you'd love to keep her yourself?" Grandpa asked. He knew Mandy's habit of caring for all waifs and strays. "And I expect your mom and dad have had to say no?"

"I haven't asked." Mandy knew it was out of the question, not because her mom and dad were hard-hearted but because the house would be full to overflowing with stray donkeys, rabbits, hedgehogs, pigs, owls, and lambs, not to mention dogs and cats, if Mandy had her way.

"But you'd love to find a good home for this little lady if it turns out she's been abandoned?" Grandpa guessed.

Mandy nodded. "Look at her. How could anyone turn

her away?" she repeated. The dog had lifted one paw onto Mandy's knee and gazed into her face.

Grandma sighed. "You say Adam has sent out SOS messages to try to find out who owns her?"

"Yes, but no one's called back so far. Everyone we know is passing the word around."

"Hmm. . . ." Grandma stamped her feet to keep warm. She was muffled in a red woolen scarf and a red beret. "Have you thought about taking her to Betty Hilder down at the sanctuary?" Betty ran a home for stray animals in Welford. She would be sure to find room for the sheepdog.

Mandy stood up. "Not yet. I haven't thought that far ahead. I'd better talk to James about it first, since he helped to rescue her."

Grandma nodded. "Betty's might be worth a try."

Mandy turned toward the house. "Come on, girl!" The dog stuck like glue to her side. "I don't know, Grandma. Betty would take good care of her, I know, but she doesn't have all that much space. I'd like to think of this dog getting better and running around the hillsides, like she used to. I'm sure she'd make a good working dog on a farm somewhere." She could imagine the dog, sleek and fit, ranging across the fields, her long, bushy tail streaming in the wind.

"You're probably right," Grandpa agreed, "judging by how obedient she is. And nice natured, too." They went into the unit and Mandy took her down to her kennel.

"Good girl," she said as the dog went in and lay down. "You have a rest, get your strength back." It was probably her imagination, but she thought she could already see the dog gaining weight and recovering the gleam in her eyes, the shine on her coat. Her markings were lovely, now that she was cleaned up — black ears and eye patches with a white stripe down her muzzle, a white chest, and black hindquarters.

"Do I hear the phone?" Grandma asked as they emerged into the fresh air.

Mandy dashed ahead, just in time to pick up the receiver before the phone stopped ringing.

"Ah, you are there, Mandy dear!" Mrs. Ponsonby's rich tones rang out. "Do you have a moment to spare?"

"Yes, Mrs. Ponsonby." Mandy put one hand over the phone and rolled her eyes at Grandma and Grandpa as they followed her into the kitchen. "Just be a sec!" she mouthed. Then she turned back to the phone. "How can I help? Is Pandora all right?"

"Oh, there's nothing wrong. No, Pandora's fine, thank you very much. No, this is about your little idea for a pets' Christmas party."

"Ye-es?" Mandy waited to hear what came next. Had Mrs. Ponsonby taken it upon herself to call the pastor and get him to change his mind about the village hall?

"Well, I've been thinking. As you know, I was very much against the idea at first. I'm afraid the standard of behavior among pets these days leaves much to be desired."

"Yes." Mandy kept her voice level. So far, Mrs. Ponsonby hadn't dropped any bombshells.

"Many of them have no manners, but that's because their owners have none either, especially the young ones."

"Is that so, Mrs. Ponsonby?"

"Oh, I don't mean you, Mandy dear!" Mrs. Ponsonby's singsong voice rose an octave. "Well, anyway, I've been thinking it over. Perhaps I should let Pandora and Toby come to the party after all."

"Great!" Mandy jumped in. "I'm sure they'll enjoy themselves."

Mrs. Ponsonby ignored her and sailed on. "The point is, my dear, Pandora can come and set an example to all those other badly brought up animals. She'll raise the tone of the event, if you see what I mean."

Mandy managed not to laugh. "I'm sure she will. And Toby, too."

"Yes. Now, my dear, since my little darlings will be able to come, I'd like to offer my own services in the organizational side of things. I'm sure your grandma already has enough on her plate, and if there's any way I could possibly help get things ready beforehand . . ."

Mandy's jaw dropped at the idea of Grandma accepting help from Mrs. Ponsonby. She cleared her throat. "Actually, Grandma is here now," she said. "Would you like to talk to her?"

Grandma's eyes widened. As she came across the kitchen, Mandy dropped the phone into her hand as if it were a hot potato. Soon Grandma and Mrs. Ponsonby were deep into party planning.

Mandy slipped toward the door. She grabbed her jacket from the back of a chair. "I'm out of here!" she whispered to her grandfather. "I have to meet up with James. We're going to deliver more invitations."

"Wise move," Grandpa whispered back. He nodded toward his wife, who was talking animatedly into the phone. "I'm afraid this could take some time!"

So Mandy and James biked around, handing out invitations and getting in the mood for Saturday's party.

That evening Mandy sprawled on the rug in the warm kitchen at Animal Ark, one arm around the sheepdog's neck, trying to believe even now that the phone *would* ring, and a worried owner would be reunited with a faithful pet.

But no such luck. The phone stayed silent. Mandy's one comfort, as she went to bed on that Tuesday night, was that the dog was looking much better. She'd been fed and rested, brushed, pampered, and made to feel special. After another good night's sleep, she would be almost back to normal.

The next morning, Mandy arrived in the village just in time to see James being dropped off outside McFarlane's newsstand. His dad lifted his bike out of the back of their station wagon, closed the door, and climbed back into the driver's seat. He gave a wave and drove off in the direction of Walton, the nearest town to Welford.

"Only four days to go!" James greeted her. He took off his glasses to polish them. "We'd better get a move on with these last invitations. How's the sheepdog?" he asked, all in one breath.

"Much better." Mandy waited for him to mount his bike. "She's eating like a horse."

"Great. Hey, guess what, they've forecasted snow before the weekend!" James slung one leg over the seat.

"A white Christmas!" Mandy really liked this idea. It would add an extra something to their party.

"Just so long as it's not too deep for people to get through," James warned. He was thinking ahead as usual. "Where to first? Ernie's house?"

At last they were ready for another busy morning delivering cards.

Ernie Bell lived near Walter Pickard at the end of the small row of stone row houses by the side of the Fox and Goose. He came to the door and received his invitation straight-faced. "Eh, I don't know about that," he said slowly. Sammy, the gray squirrel, sat perched on his shoulder. "Parties aren't really my cup of tea." He rubbed his grizzled white head.

Sammy puffed out his cheeks and darted across his shoulders, chattering excitedly.

Mandy laughed. "Sammy doesn't agree, do you, Sammy?"

"He likes parties!" James said.

The squirrel chattered back.

"Lydia will be there," James added. "She's bringing Houdini."

"Is she now?" Ernie was weakening, they could see.

Just then another gray head popped out from the far end of the street. It was Walter, Ernie's pal. "He'll be there, don't worry, you two. I'll see that he puts on a clean shirt and tie."

James ran along to deliver Walter's own card. "No need for that," he explained. "You can make a party hat for the competition if you like. Otherwise, come dressed however you want."

Walter grunted. "We'll think about that, young man." He pocketed his invitation and went on badgering Ernie to accept.

Sammy joined in, hopping up and down Ernie's arm. "We'll see," he said at last.

"That means yes." Walter winked at James. The two old men shut their doors, and James and Mandy went on their way, across the parking lot to the pub to find John Hardy.

"Do you think he's home from boarding school?" Mandy asked, as they knocked at the back door of the pub.

James nodded. "I saw him the other day."

When John came downstairs in his neat cream cable-knit sweater, he was delighted with his invitation. He promised to bring along both Button and Barney. "Imogen's away for the whole vacation," he explained. "I'm looking after the rabbits for two weeks." Their arrangement to share the care of the twin brown rabbits was working out well.

"At least you won't have far to come to the party," Mandy told him. "We all plan to meet up here with lanterns and flashlights, and we'll walk in a procession down to the village hall. Will that be okay?"

"Great!" John's eyes lit up. "Thanks for asking me!" He waved them on their way.

Next came Susan Collins's invitation. They found her exercising her pony, Prince, in the frosty paddock at the back of her huge house, The Beeches. Rider and horse made a perfect combination, Susan erect in her saddle, Prince beautifully groomed and healthy. Mandy could tell that Susan was genuinely pleased not to be left out of their plans. She leaned from the saddle and took her invitation. "Party hats, huh?" she said thoughtfully. "Well, we'll see what we can do!"

James and Mandy left her to ponder and rode on to Greystones Farm along the valley bottom. "Hi!" they called to Ken Hudson, at work in a nearby field. He carried food to the hardy Saddleback pigs. "Have you seen Brandon?"

"In the barn with Ruby!" he yelled back.

They went on, and sure enough, they came across the tall, gangling figure of Brandon Gill, busy forking bales of hay onto a trailer, with round, rambunctious Ruby the pig squatting on her haunches, idly watching.

Ruby turned to the barn door and spotted them, gave a small squeal, and trotted up. James bent to scratch her pink-and-black back.

Mandy held out the card to Brandon. He blushed deep red and mumbled his thanks. The envelope was quickly shoved into the pocket of his denim jacket.

"Can you come?" Mandy asked.

He nodded.

"Seven-thirty. Bring Ruby," James reminded him.

"Just try and stop her!" Brandon laughed. "You know Ruby; she gets her nose into everything!"

Ruby grunted and snuffled at James's shoes. He took one of Blackie's dog biscuits from his pocket and held it out to the pig. Ruby nibbled it delicately from his palm with her soft, velvety snout.

And then they were off again, heading on to the main road, pausing for breath at the village crossroads. "What about Claire?" James asked. "I guess she really can't bring the hedgehogs, but it would be more fun for her if she didn't have to come on her own."

Mandy thought about it. "It's a problem, I know." Little Claire McKay was devoted to her prickly winter lodgers in her hedgehog refuge, but even she would realize she couldn't disturb their hibernation to bring them to a party. For a while, Mandy was as stuck as James. "Wait, I have an idea," she said at last. "That is, if you wouldn't mind . . ."

James grinned. "Go on, Mandy. Spit it out!"

"Well, it's just a thought. Could you lend Blackie to Claire? They get along well, don't they? And that would still leave Eric for you to bring." She knew it was a big thing to ask James to trust Claire with his dog. But at least it would give him the chance to bring along his cat.

James hardly hesitated. "Fine!" he agreed.

"Oh, James, that's great! Why don't you go and tell Claire? See if she thinks it's a good idea. I'll just run over to Dorian's place and ask Andi if they can come along."

"Meet up at your place for lunch?" James asked.

She nodded. Even though preparations for the party were in full swing, there was still a lot to do. They biked off in different directions. As she headed for Manor Farm, Mandy hoped for great things; a get-together at the Fox and Goose, a Christmas card scene of snow, holly, and robins, a candlelit procession up the dark street, and mountains of food!

Five

Wednesday lunchtime arrived before Mandy knew it. She hurried home after her visit to Manor Farm to meet up with James and grab a bite to eat. To her surprise, she found her dad playing with the Border collie in the warmth of the kitchen.

"I just took her out of the unit to check her over," he explained.

But Mandy knew better; he hadn't been able to resist the dog's lovable face and trusting eyes.

"Adam, you're going soft in your old age!" Mandy's mom stood at the stove, heating a large pot of vegetable soup. She smiled as Mandy's dad rolled the dog onto her back and tickled her stomach.

"No way!" The good-natured game continued as the dog squirmed onto her feet and bounced up with her front paws against Dr. Adam's stomach. "Ouch! No, I'm just making sure she's recovered from her ordeal," he said.

"It looks as if she has." Mandy nodded and laughed. "It's great, isn't it? But have we had any word about where she came from yet?"

Dr. Adam shook his head. "A big negative on that one, I'm afraid."

Mandy sighed. "I wonder what she's called?" She went to stroke the dog's nose. "It seems wrong to just think of her as 'the dog' or 'the stray.' She must have a name that she would answer to."

"Why not give her one?" Dr. Emily suggested. She ladled hot soup into four bowls. "You and James. I think you're entitled to do that, since you were the ones who rescued her."

Mandy nodded and felt her face glow with pleasure. She waited impatiently until James arrived, then sat with him over the soup and crusty bread. The dog snoozed in a warm corner, tired out by the game, while Mandy and James made yet another list.

"Lassie . . . Jessie . . . Badger?" James suggested.

"Patch . . . Winnie . . . Sally?" Mandy tried out several names. None sounded quite right. They thought again.

"Flora?" Dr. Adam chipped in.

They shook their heads.

"Jemima, Ermintrude, Gwendolen," he suggested, rattling them off.

"Dad!" Mandy raised her eyebrows. "You can't call a dog Ermintrude!"

"Gwen wouldn't sound too bad," James added.

Mandy looked at the dog. She'd opened her eyes, head resting on her front paws, seeming to take some interest in this naming game. "Gwen?" Mandy experimented. There was no response. "How about Tess? Tess, here, girl!" she called softly.

The dog stood up and walked smartly toward her.

"Sit, Tess!"

She sat.

Mandy looked at the others in pleased surprise.

"Tess it is!" said Dr. Emily.

Everyone was delighted. "Do you think that really is her name?" James asked.

Adam Hope shrugged. "Who knows? All I can tell is, she seemed to like the idea."

"Tess suits her, doesn't it?" Mandy felt it was a good name for a working dog — short, sharp, and sturdy.

"Tess thinks so," James laughed. "You'd better watch it, Mandy. You're already her best friend." He watched the dog licking Mandy's hand and putting her head on her lap.

"Seriously," Dr. Emily agreed. "We mustn't let her get too attached. Remember, we can't keep her." She looked kindly at Mandy before she cleaned up the lunch things.

Mandy stood with a sigh. "Down, Tess," she ordered. "And we still have so much to do for the party, so I'd better get you back to the unit. That's a good dog." Quickly she led her outside through the yard to the residential unit. "Good girl," she whispered as she locked the door.

Leaving her there was hard. Try as she might to toughen up and be sensible over Tess, Mandy had to admit that the dog had touched her. In fact, she was head over heels in love with the gentle, affectionate creature.

James peered at Mandy as they pocketed the last of their invitations and set off on their bikes once more. "Are you sure you're okay?" he asked.

She nodded. "Yes, thanks. Where to now?" Her head was still in a whirl over Tess, and her heart wasn't in the task for the afternoon.

"The Spillers'," he suggested. They biked in silence toward the field, where Jack Spiller and his family worked their small plot of land. James carried an invitation for six-year-old Jenny Spiller and her pet sheep, who was also named Blackie. James seemed to be thinking long and hard. "Mandy," he said, "you don't think Jack Spiller might . . . I mean, he keeps a few sheep. . . . He might . . . want to take Tess!" At last he managed to get the words out, holding his breath for Mandy's reaction.

Mandy felt her heart give a little jolt at the new idea. She caught her own breath and pedaled silently along a flat stretch of road. The Spillers were nice people. They already had a working dog on the farm. She tried to think it through. If Tess had to go somewhere, she realized the Spillers would make good owners for her. "Let's ask," she agreed. It was better than Betty Hilder's sanctuary, and that was the only other idea they'd come up with so far.

As they arrived at the house, Jenny Spiller came running to meet them, with Blackie close on her heels. He'd already grown into a sturdy young sheep.

"And everywhere that Jenny went . . ." James laughed at the sight of the inseparable pair.

Soon Jack Spiller appeared at the door. "What brings you two up here?" he called.

James explained about the party. Jenny jumped up and down in excitement. "Can I go, Dad? Please!"

Jack Spiller readily agreed. "Thanks for asking her. I'll drive her down. Half-past seven on Christmas Eve, you say?"

Mandy stood by while James and Mr. Spiller made the arrangements. She felt her stomach turning nervously. Finally, as Mr. Spiller looked at his watch and took Jenny by the hand, she plucked up the courage to speak.

"Mr. Spiller, would you by any chance be able to take an extra dog?" she asked straight out. There seemed to be no point sidling into the issue. "We've rescued a stray, and so far no one has come forward to claim her. We need to find her a good home. James thought you might be able to do with the extra help?" She gripped her handlebars tightly and waited for the answer. The icy feel of cold metal seeped through her gloved hands.

Jack Spiller halted and turned. "A working dog?"

Mandy nodded. "A Border collie. A female. She's so gentle. We've called her Tess." She found it hard to keep her voice steady, but she was determined to do her best to find the dog a good home.

"Female?" Jack Spiller slowly began to shake his head. "That would mean we'd have two female dogs around the place," he said. "That wouldn't work, I'm afraid. They wouldn't get along. Now, if it had been a male, we might have found room for him!" He smiled at Mandy. "It's a no go, I'm afraid."

"Thanks anyway, it was just an idea," she said. Suddenly she realized how much hope she'd pinned on Mr. Spiller saying yes. Tess would have loved it up here, working for her keep.

"Sorry. Better luck next time," Jack Spiller said. He led Jenny back to the house, with Blackie trudging along behind.

Mandy sighed and looked at James. He shrugged. "Nearly," he said.

"So near and yet so far," she agreed. They set off down the hill.

"Right!" James set his jaw and sounded determined. "We're not going to let this problem ruin our Christmas, are we?"

Mandy took up the challenge. "We are not!"

"We are going to get Tess settled in a terrific new home before the party!" he insisted. He let go of his brakes on a straight downhill stretch.

Mandy followed, feeling the wind in her hair. "We are!" She began to smile as they swooped down into the valley.

"We will work this one out!"

"We sure will!"

"We will not give in!" he shouted over his shoulder. "Never!"

By the time they'd reached the bottom of the hill, Mandy had shaken off her regrets about parting with Tess. She knew they owed it to everyone to do their very best to find a home for the dog before Christmas.

Mandy's gaze swept along the road by the riverside. "Do we have time to stop by Greystones?" she asked suddenly.

"Of course. Why?" James was catching his breath after the downhill charge.

"Wait and see. It's my turn to have an idea!" she grinned. She biked ahead.

"But we gave Brandon and Ruby their invitations yesterday." James gasped to keep up. They sped between bare hawthorn hedges, still white with frost. Soon the gray square building came into view.

"I'm not looking for Brandon." Mandy put on her brakes and squealed to a halt. She came level with the field where the Gills kept their pigs. "I'm looking for Ken!"

Ken Hudson was the pigman at the farm. He was small and wiry, a no-nonsense sort of man who'd recently moved to live with his sister on her upland farm. He still worked here in the valley at Greystones Farm. James spied him now, crossing the field between the arched shelters where the black-and-white pigs lived and fed. He carried two buckets of food and whistled as he walked. "There he is!" James pointed to him empty-ing the buckets into a metal trough.

Mandy spotted him, too. She laid down her bike and jumped over the wall into the field. Several pigs came running toward her, including Napoleon, the huge, friendly boar. "Hi, Ken!" She waved both arms, glad to see him put down his empty buckets and stride down-hill. James joined her, and together they scratched the backs of the pigs and let them root around their feet.

"Now, then, what can I do for you?" A smile wrinkled up Ken's thin face. He shifted Napoleon out of the way with a hefty shove and stood with hands on hips, his cap tilted back on his head.

"Merry Christmas, Ken!" Mandy grinned. She liked Ken. His looks reminded her of a wizened jockey, skinny and bowlegged in his black rubber boots.

"No, you haven't come all this way just to wish me Merry Christmas," he countered. He looked quizzically at Mandy.

"We came to see how your move went," Mandy con-tinued. "Didn't we, James?"

"Yes!" He gave her a sideways look.

"It went like clockwork." Ken scratched his forehead. "I didn't have much stuff to move. Got it all up to the farm in one trip and settled in just great. Dora's been fattening me up since I went to live with her."

"That's good." Mandy shifted from one foot to the other.

"And?"

"And what?" She opened her eyes wide.

"And what else can I do for you?" Ken half-smiled. "You can't fool me; you're up to something, Mandy Hope!" He turned to James. "She is, isn't she?"

"Search me." James tried to look innocent. But he gave Mandy a quick shove.

"You like dogs, don't you, Ken?" Mandy had decided the best tactic this time was to go slow and easy.

"I like everything that goes on four legs," he answered. Napoleon nudged against him, sniffing at his pocket. Without thinking, Ken dipped in his hand and offered the boar a wrinkled windfall apple.

"You'd like Tess, then." Mandy gazed up at the frosty hillside, a plaid scarf knotted around her neck, her green jacket zipped tight.

"Who's Tess?" Ken filled the pause.

"Tess is a great dog, isn't she, James? Super friendly. And she does everything you tell her. She's a black-and-white Border collie with big brown eyes. I'm sure she could be a champion dog!"

"Whose dog is she, then?" Ken sounded interested.

"Ah!" Mandy held the suspense.

"I haven't heard of a new dog around here," he insisted. "She sounds like she might be something special!"

"She is! Would you like to see her?" Mandy felt him grab the bait. She knew Ken wouldn't be able to resist the build-up she'd given the dog.

"Maybe." He considered it, his head to one side.

"Why don't I bring her over?" Mandy offered.

But Ken shook his head. "Not here. I'm heading home now, up to Dora's place. I've finished work for the day."

"Well, we could bring her up. In fact, we'd love to. We could put her through her paces for you, if you like. She's great to watch."

"She is, is she?" Ken looked suspiciously at Mandy. "A wonder dog?"

At last Mandy decided to come clean. "The fact is, she needs a new home. I thought you might take her." Again she held her breath.

"You did?" As usual, Ken answered with a question. Mandy nodded.

Ken tugged at the peak of his cap. He looked down at his boots. "A new home?" he repeated.

"Tess is a stray. James and I rescued her. She really is a fantastic dog, Ken! I'm sure you'd love her!"

Ken studied Mandy's eager face. "A Border collie? A champion?"

"I'm sure she could be! You could train Tess to do anything. What she needs is a place where she could be put to work rounding up sheep. You have to take a look at her and see!"

"Maybe there's room for another dog alongside Whistler," Ken admitted. "Now, I don't know what Dora would say, but . . ."

"We can bring Tess up to show you!" Mandy couldn't contain her excitement. She ran up to Ken, her face shining.

He nodded. "Why not?"

James whooped and jumped up.

"Bring her up first thing tomorrow. Let's have a look at this marvelous sheepdog," he told Mandy. "After all, I can't see any harm in taking a look, can you?"

Six

To the outsider, Dora Janeki's sheep farm was a miserable place, cut off by steep hills and bare expanses of brown, wintry grass. But it was sheep farm country, wild and unwalled, where sheep grazed in the distance and the dogs ran far and wide.

Tess sat in the back of the Animal Ark jeep with Mandy and James at her side. Dr. Adam had offered to drive them up to meet Ken Hudson early on Thursday morning, before he began his rounds. "I'll pick you up on the way back," he said as he came to open the back door. Tess jumped down and sniffed the grass, her tail curving up in an elegant arc. It had a white tip that seemed to float among the low brown tufts. "Don't expect her to do too much," he warned them. "She's still building up her strength, remember."

Mandy nodded. "Thanks, Dad. See you later."

She and James jumped down after Tess. The weather had turned cloudy, with a strong, cold wind. It was one of those winter days when it seems it will never get fully light. Mandy pulled her plaid scarf around her chin and whistled Tess to heel.

"Good luck!" Adam Hope jumped back into the driver's seat and leaned out. "I'll keep my fingers crossed!"

They waved him off, then turned to tramp up a bridle path to Syke Farm. Sensing the freedom of the open spaces, alert and eager, Tess loped beside them until they reached the bare farmyard. Then James went ahead to knock at the faded red door of the house.

Mandy kept Tess back as she watched Dora Janeki come to the door. She spotted Whistler, the farm dog, peering out of his kennel at the far side of the yard. He was a tall, rangy animal, with a long gray coat. He was speckled all over with small patches of black, and his left ear was black, too. His eyes were a strange pale gray color, almost white. Now she saw his hackles rise, and he growled as he spotted Tess.

"Yes?" Mrs. Janeki looked suspiciously at James. Small and skinny like her brother, but without Ken's friendly smile, she was a short-tempered woman with sharp, poker-straight features. Mandy knew her reputation as a worrier and a skinflint, and realized now that she certainly didn't welcome visitors.

"Hello, I'm James Hunter. We've come to see Ken," James explained.

Dora grunted. "That's the first I've heard of it. Are you sure?" She quieted Whistler with a sharp word and frowned at the newcomers.

"He asked us to bring Tess up to see him." Mandy put Tess on a lead and walked forward. "He said he'd like to take a look at her."

"Did he, now?" The frown deepened. "I can't think why. Wait here."

She closed the door abruptly and vanished. Mandy felt her hopes dive as they stood in the cold, wintry yard.

But they revived when Ken emerged, wrapped up against the weather in a high-necked thick green sweater and a big blue duffel coat, wearing his cap low on his forehead. He closed the door behind him and stamped his feet. "You've come at a good time," he said, glancing at Tess. "So, this is her." He began to walk around her in a slow, wide circle.

"Sit, Tess!" Mandy felt the dog stir uneasily. A few yards off, Whistler kept up his low growl. "Stay, girl," she said quietly, praying that Tess would submit to Ken's inspection.

Ken walked full circle, then came up to them. "Thin as a rake," he commented, still staring down at Tess.

"You'd be, too, if you'd been through what Tess has just been through." Hurriedly Mandy described the dog's long, cruel walk; how they'd found her weary, starved, and footsore, on the very point of collapse. Through the story, Tess sat quiet, one eye on Whistler, waiting for the next command.

"She's not strong, then?" Ken bent to run his hand down Tess's long black-and-white coat.

"She soon will be," Mandy promised. "She's getting the best treatment. We're building her up on food and vitamins. And she's tough. You'd be amazed at how quickly she was back on her feet"

"Hmm." Ken crouched down. The dog looked back at him curiously. "And she'll do anything you tell her?"

"Yes. Do you want to see?"

Ken gave her a brief nod.

"Stay, Tess!" Mandy gave the clear order. Then she and James moved off across the yard. Tess sat still as a statue, with Ken looking on. "Here, Tess!" Mandy called. Tess bounded forward and joined them in a flash.

"Let's try something else," Ken suggested. He scouted

around for a piece of broken branch from the bare horse chestnut tree that overhung the yard.

"Good girl, Tess!" Mandy breathed. She held up crossed fingers to show James.

"Great," James agreed. He patted the dog and stood up to see what the next test would be.

Ken came across with a stick. "See if she'll fetch this when you tell her."

Mandy took the stick and showed it to Tess. The dog sniffed and frisked up at it. Then Mandy turned away from the house and threw the stick toward the field with all her might. "Fetch, Tess!" she called.

And the dog was gone, streaking through the grass as the stick arched through the air. She bounded out of sight. The stick landed. Tess reappeared with it clamped between her jaws. Quickly she ran back to Mandy and dropped it at her feet. Then she sat, front paws neatly together, head up, panting, her tongue lolling out.

"Good girl." Mandy smiled with relief. She turned to Ken.

He nodded. "Not bad. Now let's take her up on to the hill and see how she gets along with the sheep, shall we?" He led the trek across country toward four or five distant white specks.

James and Mandy struggled to match the tough little farmer's pace, but Tess loped easily, seeming to know exactly what was expected of her now.

"I only hope she can do this!" James whispered to Mandy. "You don't think we're expecting too much?"

Mandy's own heart was in her mouth, as eventually they came to a stretch of short, firm grassland. The sheep were now in the near distance, a couple of hundred yards up the slope.

"Right," Ken said. "Step aside, you two. Let's see what she can really do." He gave a low, short whistle. Tess pricked up her ears and glanced at Mandy. Then she trotted to Ken and sat, waiting.

Ken gave a second whistle, higher and longer. Tess leaped to her feet and ran straight as an arrow toward the group of grazing animals. He whistled again, a piercing sound that rose high at the end. Tess's track curved to the right, around the back of the sheep. Ken gave a blast of short, sharp whistles. She circled around and around, drawing the sheep into a tight cluster.

"Wow!" James stared openmouthed. "She's good!"

Then Ken's call altered. The note was lower. He was calling Tess back. She hustled and darted, heading off the front sheep, slowing turning the bunch toward Ken and driving them downhill. She brought them back without faltering once.

Wild-eyed, the sheep clustered around Ken. He called to Tess to heel. The sheep scrambled away, free to take up their grazing farther down the hillside. Mandy and James ran up to Ken and Tess. "Well?" they said, impatient for his verdict.

At his feet, Tess crouched low. Her sides heaved like bellows; her pink tongue lolled sideways. "Too much like hard work, huh?" Ken muttered.

"Well?" Mandy couldn't restrain herself a moment longer. "What do you think?"

Ken looked up. "It's not so much what *I* think. It's what the boss thinks." He gave a wry nod toward the house. "Dora has the final say around here."

"But what do *you* think?" Mandy insisted. She felt the wind blow from behind. Flakes of snow began to drift from the dark sky.

Ken paused. He bent to reward Tess with a firm pat against her side. "Champion," he confirmed. "If it were up to me, I'd take her like a shot!"

Tess wagged her tail. Mandy grinned at James.

"What will your sister say?" James asked. "Will she agree?"

Ken shrugged and looked down toward the house. "Here she comes now. Why not ask her yourselves?"

They turned in surprise to see Dora Janeki striding toward them in a long blue overcoat, wearing a checked brown scarf tied firmly around her head. She didn't smile as she approached, hands in pockets, shoulders hunched. "Can't you see it's snowing?" she complained. "Do you want me to call out the snowplows to get you two back home?"

Mandy swallowed. James frowned. Ken grinned. "You watched that, didn't you?" He went down to meet her. "I saw you looking out of the bedroom window as I was putting her through her paces. I knew you couldn't keep your nose out of it for long!"

Dora sniffed. "I don't know what you mean."

"What did you think?" Ken insisted.

"About what?"

"Oh, pull the other one, Dora!" Ken enjoyed teasing her. "You saw Tess at work, all right. Mandy and James here want to know what you thought of her."

Dora looked up at the snow clouds, she frowned at Mandy, she told her brother off for going behind her back, she grumbled about the cost of taking on another dog. But in the end, she gave in. "She's all right, I suppose," she admitted grudgingly. "Considering we don't know a thing about her."

"*All right!*" Ken retorted. "She's wonderful!" Again he patted and fondled Tess.

"And you'll keep her?" Mandy could hardly believe it.

"That depends on how much you want for her," Dora said with narrowed eyes.

"Nothing."

"Nothing?" It was Dora's turn not to believe her ears.

"We just want you to give her a home," Mandy assured her.

"And something useful to do," James added.

"In that case," Dora said, speaking in a rush before they could change their minds, "we'll have her, thank you very much!"

"She can stay?" James and Mandy asked together.

Dora Janeki nodded once and turned on her heel. Ken Hudson slapped his thigh and grinned. Mandy grabbed James's arm and danced around in a circle. Tess jumped up and joined in.

"I won't tell you again — it's snowing!" Dora yelled at them. "Don't expect me to get up a rescue party!"

Ken laughed. "Come on, she's right. We'd better get you back down." Together they went to the farm to wait for Dr. Adam. "My sister's bark is worse than her bite," he whispered as they walked. "She's really taken to Tess, only she doesn't like to show it."

Mandy nodded. They had what they wanted. Tess had a home. She would be out on the hillsides where she belonged. Ken was the best; he would be firm and kind, and look after her for the rest of her life. Tess would never again be found abandoned and starving.

But as she stood in the farmyard, watching the jeep wind its way through the flurry of snowflakes and wind, Mandy's heart felt torn in two. Yes, she wanted Tess to stay up on the wild hill with Ken Hudson. But deep inside, it hurt to leave her. As she bent to give Tess one last hug, the dog's soft black nose nuzzled against her cheek. She put her paw on Mandy's lap and growled softly.

"Come and see her whenever you like," Ken said quietly.

Mandy stood up with a lump in her throat, feeling the snowflakes settle and melt on her cheeks. Wondering which were tears and which was snow, she nodded quickly, turned, and walked away.

Seven

"Well done!" Adam Hope said as he stopped to pick up Mandy and James on the lonely road by Syke Farm. Tess was nowhere to be seen. Snowflakes whirled around and settled on them, then melted into glittering drops on their hair and jackets as they climbed into the warm car. "I take it Ken said yes?"

Mandy nodded. She didn't trust herself to say anything as they set off, the jeep's thick, wide tires firmly gripping the snowy surface. The wipers worked hard to keep the windshield clear.

"I hope this weather doesn't set in." Dr. Adam glanced at Mandy. "Snow may be pretty to look at and all that, but it makes a vet's job twice as difficult, and the animals don't like it much either."

"The forecast says it'll clear later in the day," James reported.

From the flat conversation, Mandy could tell that they, too, were feeling the absence of Tess's friendly face in the back of the car.

They drove on for a while in silence. Then, as Welford village came within sight and Dr. Adam turned to go down their street, he remembered a message for Mandy. "Oh, Grandma asks if you two can go and meet her at the village hall as soon as you get back. She wants to talk to you about decorations or something like that."

Mandy nodded.

Her dad braked and stopped. "Should I drop you here to save you a walk?" He looked closely at her. "It's best to keep busy," he advised. "It'll help keep your mind off Tess."

She smiled. Her dad always had a knack of knowing what was on her mind. "Thanks, Dad. Good idea. We'll see you later."

"Could you call my mom and tell her where I am, please?" James jumped out into the cold air. Already the snow seemed to be lighter, the sky clearer.

Dr. Adam said he would, so together James and Mandy jogged back into the village, heading for the hall.

When they arrived, they stamped the snow off their boots and opened up the big oak door. Inside, Grandma greeted them cheerily from halfway up a stepladder. Rolls of colored paper streamers, glittering gold stars, and packages of balloons lay scattered over the floor. Grandpa was busy wedging a six-foot-high Christmas tree into a wooden barrel in the far corner of the big room, while Ernie Bell stood offering advice. "Left a bit, now right a bit; right, right, left a bit!" he barked, until at last the tree stood perfectly straight.

"See those balloons?" Grandma asked. She pointed to the packages on the floor. "Your young lungs are stronger than ours. See how many you can blow up, while I try hanging these streamers."

Mandy and James set to work, blowing with all their might. Soon their cheeks ached and they ran out of breath. One balloon burst with a hollow bang. But the floor came alive with floating red, yellow, blue, orange, and white balloons of all shapes and sizes.

Meanwhile, Grandma fought the streamers. She straightened out the tangles and pinned thumbtacks into hard, wooden rafters. Then she came down the ladder and draped the streamers across the room, from corner to corner, with James's help. Grandpa and Ernie were by now busy with tinsel and lights, decorating the beautiful tree.

At last Mandy blew up the final balloon. James had collapsed on the floor, head propped against the wall, surrounded by the multicolored sea of balloons.

"Let's gather them up and attach them to pieces of string," Mandy gasped. She began to crawl on her hands and knees, chasing after them as they floated out of reach.

"That's the idea!" Grandma said. "We can hang them up around the walls."

But just then the outer door opened and a gust of wind whirled in and scattered the balloons. Mrs. Ponsonby's voice "whoo-hoo"ed through the hall. Grandpa and Ernie cringed and carried on with their tree. Pandora came in, yapping excitedly. Toby stood at the door and growled in confusion. Soon both dogs pounced into the midst of the whirling balloons.

"Hello!" Mrs. Ponsonby slammed the door shut. "Dorothy? Mandy? Is anyone there?" She peered through her steamed-up glasses, putting a pointed heel firmly through a red balloon. It popped and the dogs ran in circles, barking loudly. "Oh!" Mrs. Ponsonby's hand flew to her ample chest. "Oh, my!" Pandora yapped and charged at the balloons.

"Here I am!" Grandma called from the top of her ladder. Mandy could tell she was gritting her teeth. "What can I do for you?"

"Oh, no, no! What can *I* do for *you*?" Mrs. Ponsonby swept off her heavy tweed coat and scattered more balloons. She flung it across the back of a wooden chair, then rolled up her sleeves. Then she spied Grandpa and Ernie hard at work on their tree. "Ah," she said, "it looks as if I arrived just in the nick of time!" She bustled across the room. "I always say men have no idea how to decorate a Christmas tree! They fling the tinsel on any old how. It has to be *arranged*, just so!" She pushed Ernie to one side and grabbed a piece of silver tinsel from Grandpa. "And these lights!" she said scornfully. "Just thrown on! Look, you have two pink ones together, and *three* blue ones! You need to *rearrange* them!"

Ernie and Grandpa looked at each other and retired, hurt. "Let her get on with it, if she's so eager to," Ernie grumbled. He took his cap from his pocket and went off in a huff to the Fox and Goose.

Grandpa coughed and made his excuses. "I have to slip down to McFarlane's for a roll of tape." He, too, shuffled off.

Mrs. Ponsonby nodded. "Men!" she said. She went on happily dismantling their tree.

While Dr. Emily stayed up her ladder, well out of reach, and James went on chasing stray balloons, Pandora fought on. Another balloon popped. Mandy lay flat on the floor, chin in her hands, staring Toby in the face. The scruffy mongrel had resigned himself to a long wait for his mistress. He stared back at Mandy, his mouth stretched wide in a patient, long-suffering smile. She giggled. Balloons drifted past. "Merry Christmas, Toby!" she laughed.

The dog lifted his head and gave one sharp bark.

"Ah, there you are, Mandy, my dear!" Mrs. Ponsonby sang out. "Yes, and a Merry Christmas to you, too. Oh, it's so lucky that I came to help when I did. How would you ever have gotten everything ready for the party without me?"

By Thursday lunchtime, James had managed to escape to his house. "See you later," he told Mandy. Mrs. Ponsonby was still going strong, helping to *arrange* clusters of balloons along the walls. "I told my mom I'd be back by one. She wants me to go Christmas shopping with her in Walton."

"Lucky!" Mandy whispered back. She held up an armful of balloons to Mrs. Ponsonby. "I still have to stay here for a while."

It wasn't until one-thirty that Mrs. Ponsonby was finally satisfied with the decoration of the hall. Mandy, her grandmother, and Mrs. Ponsonby stood back to admire their work, then Grandma showed them out and was able to lock the door and drive Mandy back to Animal Ark. "Don't say a word!" she warned her granddaughter. "If you even mention that dreadful woman's name, I shall explode like . . . Mount Vesuvius!"

Mandy sat beside her and laughed out loud. "But the hall does look great," she pointed out. "Looks really Christmassy!" She felt a flutter of excitement as the day for the party approached.

"Only two days to go!" Grandma said as she stopped the car and dropped her off.

Mandy nodded and dashed into the house in high spirits. She was starving and wanted to tell her mom and dad of the progress they'd made at the hall. "The party is going to be great!" she promised. She stopped in her tracks. "Hey, I just remembered — I've never given you an invitation!" She stood, poised over the cups of tea she'd just poured. "You will be able to come, won't you?"

Her parents sat and laughed at her. "Try and stop us!" they chorused.

Mandy gave them their tea, smiling happily.

* * *

In spite of Christmas, business went on as usual that afternoon at Animal Ark. First, Emily Hope was called out by the Canine Defense League. One of their men needed help with a dog who had been left at home alone by its owners. Neighbors had called to help the animal, but it was too distressed for one person to handle. Willingly, she volunteered to go lend a hand.

Adam Hope shook his head. "Sometimes I think they should ban Christmas for owners like that," he said angrily. They listened as Dr. Emily drove off in her four-wheel-drive.

It made Mandy think of Tess. "I wonder how she's doing with Ken?" she said out loud.

"Who, Tess?"

She nodded. "I hope she settles in okay."

"She will," Dad assured her. "I'd trust Ken with any animal of mine. He knows everything there is to know. And sometimes I think he prefers them to people."

Mandy sighed. "You're right. Can I come and help you this afternoon?" She followed him from the kitchen into the empty reception area.

"I was about to ask if you had time," he confirmed. "Grab a white coat. Let's help Simon clean out the residential unit before we start office hours. We only have half an hour. Let's go!"

So Mandy went and said hello to Simon. She got engrossed in her favorite work, lifting cats out of their cages and putting them gently into baskets while she cleared trays and put in food, milk, and clean newspaper. Then there were dogs to exercise and groom, the floors to sweep and disinfect. They finished work with five minutes to spare before Jean was due in reception. The phone was ringing, and Mandy headed quickly back into the office.

She picked up the phone, ready to slip in an appointment or arrange visits. She hardly expected the bad news that was about to break.

"Animal Ark. How can I help?" she said brightly.

"This is Dora Janeki here," the voice snapped back. "I need you to send someone up double-quick!"

"Yes, Mrs. Janeki." Mandy took up a pen, ready to scribble down the details.

"This is an emergency. I have a sheep here who's in a bad way. There's not a scratch on her as far as I can see. Only something's scared her and she won't let us near. She's one of my pregnant ewes. I don't like the look of it."

"Okay." Mandy jotted it down. "Do you want me to send someone straight to the house?"

"No. I'll be up on the hill, waiting. She's gone down just by the wall, past High Cross. Her legs have given way, and she may not last much longer. Can you come quickly?" Dora slammed down the phone.

Mandy thought quickly. She was just about to dial her mother's car phone when she heard the car pull up in the yard. Mandy ran out and told Emily Hope the news face-to-face.

Dr. Emily leaned out of the window. She looked serious. "Want to hop in?" she asked Mandy as she revved the engine and turned the car around the way she'd just come.

Mandy jumped right in beside her mother. They were off again, headlights glaring, speeding up the narrow roads to Dora Janeki's isolated farm.

"A pregnant ewe?" Dr. Emily swung the steering wheel to take a sharp bend. Mandy clung to the handhold.

"Yes. That's bad, isn't it?"

Her mom nodded. "It can be. It depends. If the shock's great enough, it can cause the sheep to go into premature labor."

"So she'll have the lamb too early?"

"Yes, and that can give problems to the mother, too. Internal hemorrhaging. In other words, she could bleed to death."

Mandy gripped the handle and swung from side to side. She searched the hillside for Dora Janeki. "There!" She spotted an old red four-wheel-drive van in the distance. Dr. Emily swung her car off the road, across a rough, open path toward the van.

As she saw them approach, Dora Janeki ran across the hill to meet them.

Dr. Emily and Mandy jumped down. "How bad is it?" Emily Hope asked.

"Come and see for yourself." Dora shook her head. She led them twenty yards uphill to a low, crumbling stone wall. In its lee, out of the harsh wind, lay a matted gray shape. It had a swollen belly and sticklike legs. It was lying there too weak to stand.

"Can you do anything for her?" Dora turned anxiously to Dr. Emily.

"I'm not sure yet. Let's see if we can get her back on her feet, for a start."

The three of them gently tried to ease the ewe into a standing position. But her legs buckled, and her neck and head sank against the ground. They gave up and stood by to let Dr. Emily continue her work.

"It's premature labor, all right." She swiftly examined the swollen abdomen. Then she opened her bag and worked quickly to help with the delivery. Mandy watched. She could see that the sheep was already too feeble to help herself. It was with a heavy heart that she watched her mom deliver the tiny, dead lamb.

"Stillborn," Dr. Emily murmured. "And it doesn't look too good for the mother either." She used a stethoscope to listen for the heartbeat. It confirmed that the sheep was suffering from heart failure and probably from internal bleeding. Soon Dr. Emily packed away her instruments and stood up. The animal lay completely still. "I'm sorry, Dora," she said. "There was nothing I could do."

Mandy stared at her mom. They stood helpless on this bleak hillside, and she felt weighed down by their failure.

Dora Janeki nodded. "Thank you for coming. I knew from the start we'd be lucky to save her."

Emily Hope zipped up her bag. "We gave it a try. What happened to her, do you know?" She was walking Dora back to her van.

"I can't say for sure. I brought Whistler up with me to drop off some winter feed. He was the one who found her. Something had terrified the poor beast. But by the time I got here, whatever it was was long gone."

"And do you know how long she'd been there?"

"Not really. Not overnight; I know that for sure. We were up here yesterday, rounding them up, and Whistler would've spotted her then." Dora opened the back door of her four-wheel-drive and let the dog jump down. "Wouldn't you, boy?" Dora's voice softened, and then she straightened up. "Well, that's that, I suppose." She shook Dr. Emily's hand and arranged to send a check for the bill.

"I really am sorry," Mandy's mom frowned. "I know you could do without this just before Christmas. And it's bound to set everyone else wondering."

Dora nodded. "There'll be a scare now," she admitted. "And who can blame them? Something frightened this sheep to death, and no farmer around here will rest easy until we find out what did it!"

"I'll keep my ears open," Dr. Emily promised.

She and Mandy watched Dora start up the engine. "Ken will come back up with me when he gets home," Dora said. "He'll help me tidy things up." She sighed. "Let's hope it's a one-time thing. We don't want any more of these in the days before Christmas!"

There was nothing they could say. She eased away over the farm track, leaving them to walk back to their own car.

"Well, that's that, as Dora says," Emily Hope said sadly. She glanced once more up the hillside.

Mandy knew that her mom hated to admit defeat. "Would it have made any difference if we'd gotten here sooner?"

"Who knows? But it didn't look to me as if that sheep would have survived the shock in any case. Her heart was affected. And the lamb was too little to have any chance at all. No, I don't think anything could have saved them."

Mandy felt cold and shaky as she climbed into the car. "But what could have done this?" she asked. "What sort of thing could it be?"

"A dog, most probably. That's the usual thing. That's why the farmers will all be up in arms. They'll say it's a dog from the village, or even from Walton. They'll blame someone from town for not keeping his dog under control. When word gets around, I wouldn't be surprised if they're all out with their guns, scouring the countryside for the culprit."

"A dog?" Mandy found it hard to believe that a tame pet could do this amount of damage.

"Yes." Dr. Emily slung her bag into the back and set off down the hill. The car bumped and swayed. "It doesn't even have to be a very big dog to worry a sheep to death."

Mandy sighed. "Let's hope it doesn't happen again, then."

"It's Dora Janeki I feel sorry for. She can't afford to lose livestock like this. She has a struggle to make ends meet as it is."

Mandy sat in silence. In her mind, she saw a picture of men with shotguns fanning out across the wintry hillside, scouring the fields and rocky outcrops for the rogue dog that had killed Dora Janeki's ewe. She went to bed that night with the image still clear. She dreamed of a dark shape hurtling at the defenseless sheep, fangs bared, springing out of nowhere. When she woke up in the morning, the telephone was ringing and she feared the worst.

Sure enough, there was another possible incident. Adam Hope had taken the call and hung up before Mandy had clambered into her robe and raced downstairs.

"That was Ken Hudson on the phone," he reported. His face looked worried. "He says a sheep from Jack Spiller's farm has just been brought in suffering from shock. Like before, there was no visible damage, but the poor thing was scared half to death. Jack managed to revive it by himself, and the sheep's out of danger. But the word's out. There's not a farm in the area that's not on alert."

"But why did Ken call you?" Mandy asked. "If it wasn't one of their sheep?"

Dr. Adam shook his head. "Can you take some bad news, love?" He led Mandy to a chair by the kitchen table. "Now sit down and listen to this."

"What is it, Dad?" Mandy felt her throat go dry. She looked up into his face. "Tell me, quick!"

"Ken called me because in a way he's involved. Or at least he thinks he might be, and he thought we should know." He paused. "The fact is, Dora has been putting two and two together. She's worked out that this sheep-worrying only began yesterday when Ken agreed to keep Tess at the farm. She's come to the conclusion that the dog might not be reliable; they know nothing about where it came from or how it might have been mis-treated in the past. She says a dog like Tess could easily turn."

Mandy shook her head. She looked up in disbelief. "Not Tess!" she said. She just knew in her heart that Tess couldn't possibly be responsible.

"No, but you can see how Dora might see it that way," Dr. Adam pointed out. "Ken himself doesn't know what to think. He just called us to warn us what was going on."

"It can't be Tess! It can't be!" Mandy would not be-lieve it. "Tess wouldn't do that!"

Adam Hope sighed. "It's not me you have to convince, honey!" He went slowly off to tell his wife the latest de-velopment.

"I have to talk to Dora!" Mandy said to herself as soon as he'd gone. She jumped up. "Dora has to understand that Tess would never do this! She has to stop spreading rumors about her!"

She ran upstairs to scramble into her clothes. She called James and met him in the village. By nine o'clock they were on their bikes and pedaling toward the farm. The mission was to save Tess from the farmers and their guns!

Eight

There was no sign of Dora Janeki's red four-wheel-drive in the farmyard when Mandy and James arrived. Whistler's kennel was empty, too.

"They must be up on the hill," James said. "Let's head on up there and try to find her."

But Mandy leaned one arm on the gate and stood to catch her breath. "Do you think she's taken Tess with her?" She longed for a glimpse of the dog, to make sure she was still safe and well.

James looked at Mandy. "I suppose you want to check?"

She nodded. Quickly they vaulted the steel bars of the gate and ran across the yard, "Let's try the house first," Mandy suggested. She went and knocked loudly at the faded door.

As they waited, they felt a cold north wind bite through their jackets. There was no reply. James shook his head. "She must have taken both dogs."

"Shh!" Mandy warned. She strained to listen, convinced she could hear a faint whining sound. It came not from the house but from the stone barn next door. She beckoned James toward the tall, windowless building. "I think Tess might be in here!" she whispered.

James caught the sound. "There's definitely something in there!" He pushed at the huge wooden door. It was locked. The whining grew louder.

"That's Tess. I know it is!" With a thumping heart, Mandy searched the length of the barn for a way in. Gradually the whining grew into a series of small yelps as the dog heard their footsteps and their search for another door.

"Here's one!" James had investigated the far side of the barn and found a narrow entrance, a kind of shed door. He pressed down the latch. The door swung open. "This way, Mandy!" he called.

She ran to join him, and together they entered the

dusty gloom. They heard a chain rattle on the stone floor, a dog barking out a welcome. Tess had recognized them and strained on her metal leash to greet them.

"Tess!" Mandy ran forward and dropped to her knees. She flung both arms around the dog's neck. Tess leaned against her, furiously wagging her tail.

"At least she's still okay," James breathed. He crouched to their level to look Tess over.

Mandy nodded. "But they've chained her up, poor thing. Why did they have to do that?" She examined the length of heavy, rusty chain ten or twelve feet long, attached to the wall at one end by a sturdy ring. Mandy saw that Tess wore a new leather collar and that the other end of the chain was attached to this by a strong steel clip. Steadily she stroked the dog until Tess grew calm.

"It's not hurting her." James tried to keep a clear head. "I bet it's to stop the other farmers from finding her. If they knew where she was, or if they found her roaming around, who knows what they'd do to her?"

"But look at her. Who would she attack? Poor Tess wouldn't harm a fly!" Softly Mandy stroked the gentle dog's head. Her black nose pushed against Mandy's chest and nuzzled up to her warm scarf. The white tip of her tail waved to and fro. "It's all right, Tess," Mandy whispered. "Let me take this horrible thing off!" Carefully she unclipped the chain and let it drop to the floor.

Tess shook herself all over and trotted in a pleased fashion up and down the empty barn. She sniffed here and there into hidden corners. James ran to check that the door was closed.

But as he tried to push the latch down firmly, he felt someone resist from the other side. Shocked, he stepped back. He squinted against the flood of daylight as the door was flung open. A figure blocked the doorway.

"What the heck's going on here?" a voice demanded.

"Ken!" Mandy recognized him. She ran to the door. "It's us, Mandy and James! We came to check that Tess was okay! We're sorry. We tried to ask permission, but no one came to the door."

Ken stepped in, holding the door half open. He kept a careful eye on Tess. "You took her off the chain," he said with a frown, as his eyes got used to the dark.

"Just for a few minutes!" Mandy pleaded. "To let her stretch her legs."

Ken nodded. "All right then. I bet Dora's up on the hill with a vanload of food. You'd better not be here when she gets back," he warned. "I came back up from Greystones myself to try and calm her down over this sheep-worrying business. She's up in arms about it, I can tell you!"

"She's really mad?" James asked. He wrinkled his nose and pushed on his glasses more firmly.

Ken nodded. "I was afraid she might do something rash, so I fed the pigs, then I came up to have a word." His warning sent tingles of fear down Mandy's spine. "What will she do?"

He shook his head and scratched the back of his neck. "I don't know yet. She hasn't made up her mind. But she's fixed on Tess here as the culprit." Tess had gone over to James and poked her face against him.

"And once Dora has made up her mind, nothing can change it."

Mandy let out an exasperated cry. "But just look at Tess, Ken! She's gentle as anything. How could anyone think she frightens sheep?"

He sighed and blew the air out through his thin cheeks. "They can fool you. They might look completely harmless, like Tess does now. But you turn your back for a minute, and something comes over them. They get it into their heads to go after the sheep. It's a kind of mad streak that gets into a dog."

Mandy went and stood by James and Tess. "But not into Tess!" she insisted. "Dora's wrong, I know she is!"

Ken looked anxiously at the trio, Mandy, James, and Tess. "But there *is* the fact that we don't know anything about her," he pointed out. "She could have a whole history of being unreliable that we don't know about. Maybe that's why the last owners got rid of her."

Mandy heard the words, but she wouldn't let them sink in. "No!" She blocked her ears with both hands. Still Ken's muffled voice came through.

"Then there's the fact that no sheep was attacked before she came. Now we've had two in twenty-four hours. That's what makes it look bad. *And*," he said, grinding to a decisive halt, "the fact is, Tess disappeared yesterday, when all this was going on."

His words dropped into silence.

"Disappeared?" James stood up straight. "How come?"

Ken explained. "I wasn't here, you know. But Dora says she left Tess with food and water here in the barn, to let her get used to the place. She didn't tie her up, and she went down into the village with Whistler. When she got back, the dog was missing — probably slipped off through the side door. It was swinging open when she walked in. At any rate, Tess didn't come back till well after dark. And she looked tired out, wet and cold as if she'd been outside all that time. She just curled up in a corner and fell right asleep. That's when Dora began to have her doubts."

James stared at Mandy, who shook her head. "It doesn't prove anything!" she protested.

"But on the other hand, it doesn't look good." Ken put his hands in his duffel coat pockets and sighed.

"What will Dora do?" James asked.

"I don't know yet. But I know she won't keep her on after what's happened."

Lost for words, Mandy stared helplessly at James, then at Tess. The dog seemed to have picked up the worried mood. She sat quietly in their midst, waiting patiently.

"But what actual proof does Dora have?" James found his voice. "Just because of the things you've said, it doesn't mean Tess is guilty!"

Ken shrugged. "But think about it; would *you* take the risk, with what we know?"

"Yes, I would!" Mandy cried. "Because we don't know anything! All Dora is doing is guessing." She felt like crying; the success of finding the ideal home for Tess had crumbled away to nothing. Now there was even the chance that Dora Janeki would insist on having the dog put to sleep, as a danger to livestock. Or she might let the other angry farmers of the district decide for her.

As they stood in silence, Tess let out a sharp, single bark. It echoed through the empty barn. She trotted up to the closed side door. She barked again.

"I think she wants to go out," James said. "But don't let her!"

Tess came back to them. She barked and trotted back to the door, then bounced up against the simple latch.

"Down, Tess!" Mandy ordered. The door rattled and the latch lifted slightly. Mandy went over. "Stay down, that's a good girl."

But Tess jumped and whirled, barking loudly. She ignored Mandy. Instead she lunged at the latch and released it. The door swung open. Tess bounded into the open air. She turned to wait for Mandy, then ran a few steps ahead, barked and waited.

"Stop her!" James yelled. He began to run for the door.

"Stay, Tess!" Mandy put out one arm to stop James from careering ahead. "I think she's trying to tell us something! Look, she wants us to follow!"

Tess's bark rose impatiently. She ran to the gate and stopped again, obviously meaning them to come after.

Ken emerged from the barn and shook his head. "I don't know about this. I don't think we should," he said.

"What is it, Tess?" Mandy ran ahead once more, sure that the dog had something important to show them. She turned in a tight, excited circle as Mandy approached, then slipped out between the metal bars of the gate. "What is it, girl?" Mandy said, low and tense. She glanced over her shoulder at the other two. "We have to see what she wants, at least!" she pleaded.

At last Ken gave a tight little cough and a nod. "Fair enough," he said.

Mandy swung open the gate and they followed Tess through.

Before long, Tess had led them clear of the farm buildings and up toward the hill, her black shape streaking ahead. Mandy strode after her. She realized that the day was turning gray and cold. A freezing mist descended down the hillside, and it was hard to keep Tess within sight. Even Ken's urgent whistle didn't stop her from forging ahead.

"Tess!" Mandy shouted, as a thicker cloud of mist seemed to swallow the dog from view. "Why won't she do as she's told?" She turned to Ken with a feeling of panic. Tess was so set on getting them to follow that she seemed to have lost her usual obedience and common sense. "Where are you, Tess?" she called.

They began to run up into the mist.

"Stick together," Ken insisted. "Whatever you do, don't split up. I don't want anyone getting lost!"

They called and ran until they came through the billowing mist and out the other side. The view cleared, and there was Tess, sitting on a black boulder, waiting for them to catch up.

"Good girl!" Mandy cried out in relief.

Tess put up her head and sniffed the air. Suddenly her ears pricked up. "She bounded from the rock and began to streak across the hill, once more ignoring Ken's expert call.

"Let's go!" James said. He began to race after her.

"Would you believe it, she's heading for those sheep!" Ken pointed to a few distant gray specks, grazing in the shelter of a big, rocky outcrop on the horizon.

Mandy's heart sank. She knew it was no good calling Tess back now. This is what she'd wanted to show them all along, whatever it was. Mandy chased over the rough ground after James, with Ken bringing up the rear.

They ran through another band of mist, their feet crunching over narrow, iced-up streams, the wind whipping down on them. Now Tess seemed to have forgotten they were even there, racing up the hillside; she was a low, lean, dark shape, heading straight and fast toward the unsuspecting sheep.

"No, Tess!" Mandy gave a last, desperate call. Her heart was in her mouth. She pushed herself faster and faster, unable to believe what she was seeing with her own eyes — her beautiful, gentle Tess about to attack!

But she saw the startled sheep raise their heads and skitter sideways. They bunched together as Tess approached, looking wildly in all directions. Mandy saw Tess streak up behind them, and up the almost sheer slope onto a narrow ledge of rock. The sheep trampled into one another in their alarm, bleating loudly. One went down on its front knees and skidded several yards down the hill. The others scattered for the protection of boulders, bushes, any cover they could find.

Tess towered above them on the rock. She snarled, teeth bared.

"No!" Mandy came nearer still, a hundred yards away, begging Tess to hold back.

Tess leaped. She was on the ground among the sheep, charging through them. Mandy heard a ferocious growling and snapping, bodies hurtling through bushes. She saw a sheep's terrified eyes.

Then a sharp shot rang out. Everything froze. A mist billowed across the scene, and Dora Janeki emerged, a shotgun raised to her shoulder. Whistler crouched at her heel.

Mandy caught a glimpse of Tess, lying low, but ears up, poised ready for more action.

She ran toward the woman farmer. "Oh, don't!" she pleaded.

Then the hillside seemed to come alive with men running. Two or three followed Dora's small, stern figure, shotguns at the ready. Mandy recognized Jack Spiller and Dennis Saville, the foreman at Sam Western's farm. From lower down the hill, James and Ken ran to the spot where Mandy faced Dora. Meanwhile the frightened sheep had scattered in all directions, and both Whistler and Tess lay quiet, warily eyeing the scene.

Dora stormed at her brother. "What did I say?" she shouted. "You saw that with your own eyes! I knew it was that dog right from the start!" She waved the barrel of her gun at Tess. "But you wouldn't listen!" she accused. "And I was dumb enough to hang back from doing what I knew I should do in the first place! What a fool I am!"

Ken sighed and shook his head at Mandy. "What can I do?" he muttered. "You saw it, as clear as daylight. There's the proof you were looking for!"

With the sound of the gun, Mandy had felt something snap inside her. She'd believed in Tess. Yet she'd seen her leap, teeth bared, from the rock into the midst of the sheep. The shot had rung out. It was like a nightmare. With tears in her eyes, cold and trembling, Mandy gazed silently at James.

Dora pushed them to one side and strode past, heading for Tess. Jack Spiller and Dennis Saville went to back her up. They raised their guns.

"Oh, no!" Mandy put her hands to her face.

James gripped her wrist. "Look, Mandy!" He pulled her hands away

Tess had spotted the three shapes coming menacingly toward her. She sprang to her feet and turned. Then she was off, darting up the hill into the shadow of the rocks. Three shots rang out. Still Tess fled. She vanished behind the rocks. Moments later they saw her again, making her way along the ridge. The farmers raised their guns.

Tess paused for a second, turned her head toward them, and gave a low whine. Then, with a whisk of her white-tipped tail, she vanished out of sight.

Nine

All day Friday a light snow fell. By evening, Welford lay under a crisp, white covering that sparkled in the clear moonlight. Snowplows came out to clear the roads, but the fields and hillsides lay under three or four inches of even snow.

Mandy felt numb. She'd seen Tess attack the sheep with her own eyes, and knew that Dora Janeki, Jack Spiller, and Dennis Saville would still be out on the snowy hillside with their guns. But she and James had set off for home before the snow set in, too disappointed to talk.

Ken had called Animal Ark to tell Adam Hope what had happened. Mandy's mom and dad came out to meet them. Grandma and Grandpa rallied around. They took James back to his house and persuaded Mandy to come shopping for last-minute party food. Mandy spent the afternoon and evening at Lilac Cottage, baking cakes and pastries for the party the next day.

Christmas Eve dawned bright and clear. At eight o'clock Mandy opened her bedroom curtains to a pale blue sky and a sweep of white hillsides. The bare trees were coated in thick frost, and the walls and roofs sparkled in the sunlight.

"It's a lovely day!" Emily Hope called upstairs. "Breakfast's ready!"

Mandy pulled on some jeans and a thick blue sweater, then went down for her winter breakfast of oatmeal, honey, and milk.

"It looks good for the party tonight." Dr. Emily brought a pot of tea to the table. "As long as it stays clear, there won't be any problem about getting there."

Mandy nodded. She knew there were still dozens of things to do.

"How do you feel?" Her mom put a warm hand over hers. "Do you think you'll be able to cope?" She pushed a stray strand of hair back from Mandy's face and gave her cheek a light kiss.

Mandy took a deep breath. "I'll be okay, Mom. I keep thinking of Tess, that's all."

"I know. You must be very upset."

"I never thought for a second she would do what I saw her do. In fact, I still can't believe it." Mandy shook her head. "I thought I knew her!"

"It's hard," Dr. Emily agreed. "But I think the party will help keep your mind off things, don't you?"

"Oh, yes. I don't want to let anybody down." Mandy finished her breakfast and got up from the table. "Everyone's looking forward to it. The hall's all ready, except for last-minute things. I have to stop by Simon's to help him bring the music system over and set it up. Then Grandma and Mrs. Ponsonby will start bringing the food. In fact, I'd better get going!" She reached for her jacket and scarf.

"Good for you!" Dr. Emily smiled at her. "We have a busy day in the office ourselves. See you later."

Mandy and her mom went their separate ways. Soon Mandy had met up with Simon and they were driving to the village hall in his battered white van, with the music system safely stacked in the back. They lifted it out and carried it through the open door to find Grandpa and

Ernie already putting up tables, and Grandma and Mrs. Ponsonby standing by with piles of white tablecloths.

"Wow!" Simon put down the CD player and took a look around. He saw the tree lights twinkling, the balloons, and the streamers. "This should get us all into the Christmas mood, all right!"

He plugged in wires and arranged speakers, then went off to work. James and Mr. Hunter arrived with armloads of holly from a tree in their garden. James said, "Dad thought this would look nice along the windowsills." He peered out from behind a mountain of shiny green leaves and red berries.

Mrs. Ponsonby swooped down on him and took the holly. "Perfect!" she cried. "I'll *arrange* them, just so!" She began to place the twigs and to order Mr. Hunter around. "Put those down there, would you? And the rest on that empty table, out of reach. We wouldn't want Pandora to hurt herself on those nasty prickles, would we?"

Pandora snuffled up to Mandy, who picked her up and petted her. Then she set to work helping her grandmother cover the tables with clean white cloths.

During the early part of the morning other visitors dropped by. Susan Collins offered boxes of Christmas cookies that her mom had sent. "She says there should be enough for everyone!" Susan piled the gold and silver treats into the middle of the table. "There are party hats inside for those people who don't bother to make one for the competition."

James stopped in his tracks. He put down a pile of plates with a clatter. "Uh-oh, the competition!" He suddenly remembered.

"Yes, I've already made a hat for Prince," Susan told him. "But I'm keeping it a secret."

James turned to Mandy. "I've just thought of something — we don't have anyone to judge it yet!"

"Shh!" Mandy nudged him. But it was too late.

"What's that I hear?" Mrs. Ponsonby cried. "You need someone to judge the party-hat competition? Why, I'd be glad to do it for you!" She climbed down from a chair with an armful of holly. "No need to worry about that, my dear. Let me take one more thing off your mind. Leave it to me. I'll *organize* your little competition. In fact, let me donate the prize!"

Mandy graciously accepted the offer. "I planned to ask Grandma to be the judge," she whispered to James with a grin.

"Oops, too late now!" He picked up the plates and began to set them out on the tables.

As Susan went out, John Hardy came in. "My dad wondered if you could use these," he said to Mandy. He carried a giant cardboard box full of bags of potato chips. "And there's a box of peanuts to follow." For half an hour he trooped across the street from the Fox and Goose with boxes of snacks and cans of soft drinks.

Claire McKay came next. She brought Blackie, James's Labrador, to see what was going on. She peeped around the door, her dark bangs framing her face, her brown eyes staring in delight at the preparations. Blackie ran ahead, wagging his tail at James.

"Hi, Claire!" Mandy called. "Do you want to give me a hand with these paper napkins? We have to fold them up into little hat-shaped things so they stand up, *just so!*" She grinned at James as she imitated Mrs. Ponsonby, who had just slipped out with Pandora and Toby on their "walkies."

Claire nodded and came in. She soon learned how to fold the napkins. Grandpa and Ernie finished setting up tables. Grandma was happy with their preparations. "Coffee, everybody?" she asked. She took a huge thermos flask from her shopping bag, then plastic cups, and homemade ginger cookies. "It's time for a break!"

Only now, when she had time to think, did Mandy's mind swing back to sad thoughts. As she munched her cookie, she pictured Tess, cold and miserable, cowering behind rocks, leaving telltale footprints in the new snow. Dora Janeki would be up there, too, tracking her down. She imagined a final scene — Tess shivering, her brown eyes staring down the barrel of a farmer's gun. . . .

Mandy broke out of the circle of chattering helpers. She reached for her jacket.

"Where are you off to, love?" Grandpa asked.

"Can you manage without me for an hour or so?" she asked. "There's something I'd like to do."

Grandpa looked at Grandma. They nodded. "Of course we can. We'll carry on here until you get back," he said.

"I'll come!" James jumped up. He guessed what was on her mind.

Mandy nodded. She heard him follow her out of the hall. "I'm going up to the hill," she told him quietly.

He nodded. "That's why I said I'd come." He joined her in the yard. "We'll have to walk."

"Or run." They set off at a jog up the village street. "We might not be able to save Tess," Mandy explained. "Not if the farmers have their way. But there's no need for her to suffer and die that way, not if we get to her first."

James kept pace with her. They'd cut across fields, out of the village. On the horizon, the black Celtic cross landmark showed up sharp and clear. "What are we going to do?" he asked.

Mandy ran on with her head down. Their feet crunched over untrodden snow, sinking through the frozen crust into a powdery layer below. "We're going to find her and take her back to Animal Ark before the farmers get her," she promised.

"Then what?"

Mandy stopped to stare up the hillside. "If Tess has to die because of the sheep, I'll ask my mom and dad to do it," she said. "If she's not going to be allowed to live anymore, we'll put her to sleep at Animal Ark!"

She wouldn't let Tess feel the pain of the gunshot. She wouldn't let her end her days as a hated, hunted fugitive.

They reached the tall hedges of Upper Welford Hall and had to pause again for breath. Running uphill through soft snow was hard work. They stood gasping as Sam Western's dogs barked out a warning. Then they ran on, past High Cross Farm, along the ridge where Dora Janeki's sheep usually grazed. Today it was empty, a white wonderland.

"She must have rounded them up and taken them into the barn." James gazed all around. There was no sign of life.

"Because of the snow," Mandy agreed. "But Tess is still out here somewhere. Come on!" She forged ahead through drifts of snow that had collected in hollows, searching for a dog's prints, heading for the wild rocks and hills.

"She could have frozen to death by now!" James pulled his own legs clear of a drift. He scanned the landscape.

"No!" Mandy refused to believe it. They plunged on, knee-deep in snow.

Way up in the hills, beyond Syke Farm, they stopped to look down on the scattered houses. So far they'd found no sign of Tess. But now James and Mandy thought they spotted a small group of people tramping across fields with a dog, each armed with a shotgun. It was too far away to see clearly, but they knew what it meant. The farmers' search for the rogue dog was still on.

"This way!" James dodged behind some rocks, out of sight. Mandy followed. They slid down a flat slope, over the ridge, and down the far side.

Here the snow was less deep. There was a blown scattering of powdery flakes. A strong wind had swept the hillside clean. Some sheep remained in the shelter of high rocks, still nibbling at patches of exposed grass. In this new valley, the sun had partly melted the snow and crept up the frozen slopes toward the sheep. Mandy and James slid to a halt, still deep in shadow, trying not to disturb the nervous animals.

But something else seemed to attract the sheep's attention, a sound or a smell. They glanced along the hillside, then bent to nibble the grass. Mandy held James's arm. "Wait a minute," she whispered.

She spotted a dark shape crouching low behind a far rock. It was about twenty yards from the sheep, downwind of them and creeping nearer.

Mandy longed to spring up and wave her arms in warning. She wanted to get the sheep away from the prowler. But something kept her fixed to the spot. She and James crouched and stared. The shadowy shape was a dog, and every second it crept closer to the sheep.

Nearer and nearer. The dog's back was black. Its ears and nose were pointed. It had a strong, bushy tail. But the tip wasn't white. And they could see that the belly of the dog, as it crept forward, was tan-colored. It bared its teeth, ready to pounce.

"That's not Tess!" James whispered. "It's too big!"

"It's Major!" Mandy said, her eyes wide with surprise. "It's the new dog at Upper Welford Hall!"

The German shepherd froze in its crouching position, waiting for a sheep to break from the group before he sprang.

But before anyone had time to move, Mandy felt another shape hurtle past from behind. A thin, black dog curved across the hillside between Major and the sheep, working them into a tight circle. They stopped grazing and shuffled into a tight knot. The new dog hustled them and moved them off, darting at strays, rounding them up and out of danger.

"Tess!" Mandy leaped to her feet. "She's protecting the sheep! She's trying to save them from Major!"

The rogue dog bared his teeth and snarled. He advanced on Tess from behind.

Then James ran toward the sheep, shooing them downhill toward the sunlit valley. Once on the move they ran quickly, alert and well out of reach of their attacker.

"Tess, watch out!" Mandy warned. She saw that the Border collie was in danger herself now. Major snarled again and charged at her. Tess turned to defend herself.

Major leaped at Tess. The two bodies crashed and hurtled together. They rolled down the hillside before Tess twisted free. Mandy ran at them, shouting Tess's name. Major attacked a second time. There was a yelp, more snarls and growls. "Major, get back!" she cried. Mandy stood by, helpless, as Tess struggled to defend herself.

At last the terrifying fight came to an end. Tess broke free of Major's snapping jaws, whirled on the spot, and raced away. The other dog snapped at nothing and backed off as Mandy and James moved in. A deep growl rattled in his throat. He crouched low. Then he turned tail, away from the sheep, sloping off along the side of the valley.

"Tess!" Mandy turned back up the hillside in time to see the Border collie reach the ridge and pause. "Here!"

But Tess had looked down the barrel of a gun, and she trusted no one now. She gave a quick, sharp bark, held her head high, and panted for breath. Mandy thought she met her gaze, and Tess's dark brown eyes told her that she was innocent after all.

Then she ran on out of sight, into snowy Welford valley, back toward the farmers with their guns.

Ten

Mandy knew they had to act quickly. She ran on to the crest of the hill, too late to spot where Tess had gone. But she saw her tracks running along the ridge, up the valley into the wild, hilly countryside.

James grinned as he scrambled up the slope behind her. "It isn't Tess!" he shouted. "It's a different dog!" He dipped his hands into the snow and scooped it into the air.

"She was trying to *save* the sheep! Yesterday, when we saw her in the mist and it looked like she was attacking them, she was really fighting Major, trying to keep him off. She was *protecting* them!" Mandy joined in James's celebration. "Isn't she fabulous? And the best part is that she's innocent!"

She went yelling down the slope toward Sam Western's house, half sliding, half running. "We have to tell Mr. Western about Major!" she cried. "He'll have to let the others know that it's his dog, not Tess!"

By the time they arrived at the big gates of Upper Welford Hall, Mandy and James were breathless and covered in snow. Two sturdy bulldogs came barking through the grounds toward them. A side door was flung open and Sam Western strode out.

He was dressed in a patterned sweater and brown trousers, his graying hair combed neatly to one side. He came like a true lord of the manor down his snow-covered drive.

The two bulldogs leaped at the gate, snarls on their squat faces. Mandy and James stepped back.

"What's going on?" Mr. Western looked down his nose at them. "Oh, it's you," he said coldly. "The vets' girl, isn't it?"

Mandy nodded. "And this is James. James Hunter."

"What do you want?" Mr. Western ordered the bulldogs to be quiet. "This isn't some Christmas prank, is it?" He seemed annoyed at the disturbance.

"Oh, no!" Mandy wanted to make everything clear all at once. But how did you tell someone that his dog was a sheep killer? She hesitated.

"I hope you're not carol singers. Because I don't pay carol singers, so you can pack up and be off," he warned.

"No, Mr. Western. It's about your dog Major."

A deeper frown set in. "What about Major?"

"First of all, do you know where he is right now?" James asked. He looked around the grounds, past the frozen ornamental pond, across the lawns toward the fine old house. There was no sign anywhere of the German shepherd.

Western grunted. "If you must know, he's out with my farm manager." He raised one eyebrow, ready to send them packing. "Not that it's any of your business."

"But it is!" Mandy protested. "Major must have broken free from Mr. Saville. We've just spotted him over the ridge in the next valley."

Western was caught off guard. "Darn dog," he muttered. "Why didn't you get hold of him and bring him down with you?"

"We couldn't." Mandy looked to James again for help.

"He was attacking the sheep, Mr. Western!" James came straight out with it.

The farmer let out a hard little laugh. "Nonsense!" he

began. Then he paused. "Look, I know there's a sheep attacker on the loose," he admitted. "Dora Janeki told Dennis all about it. As a matter of fact, he's out there now, helping to track it down."

Mandy and James watched Mr. Western grow red in the face. They saw a puzzled look develop.

"Major went with him, as it happens. But Major's not the villain. That's ridiculous!" He tried to bluster his way through.

Mandy looked him straight in the eye. "Where was Major on Thursday, when the first sheep were attacked?"

There was a long pause. "Now, look!" Sam Western shot her an angry glance.

Mandy stood firm. "Where was he, Mr. Western?"

"Well, he was missing for part of that day," he admitted. "Dennis had to go out in the late afternoon and round him up. But that doesn't prove anything!" He lifted his chin defiantly.

Mandy and James waited for a few moments. The two bulldogs had calmed down and began to tramp through the snow, snapping up mouthfuls and sniffing in the hedge. "But Major's on the loose again now," James said calmly. "And we've just seen some sheep being attacked. Don't you think you'd better come and check?"

Mr. Western looked sternly through the bars of the iron gates. "Wait here!" he ordered. He called to the dogs and strode off up the drive. He disappeared through the side door and closed it with a slam. Five minutes later he reappeared, dressed in green boots and a heavy jacket. His collar was turned up, and he wore a tweed hat with a curled brim, pulled well down. In one hand he carried a mobile phone, which he stuffed into his pocket.

"We'll have to be quick," Mandy said, as he came out through the gate. "The sooner we find Mr. Saville and ask him about Major, the better."

The three of them set off together along the path past High Cross Farm. They cut through a small grove of trees at the back of the empty goat field. Mandy caught a glimpse of Lydia Fawcett emerging from her barn. "Lydia, have you seen Mr. Saville?" She cupped her hands to her mouth and yelled.

"Heading up to Syke Farm!" Lydia called back.

"Thanks!" Mandy waved.

Sam Western frowned and strode ahead. "I hope this doesn't turn out to be one of your tricks," he muttered. "You'd better be telling me the absolute truth, or else!"

"We are," James promised. "You have to talk to Mr. Saville and stop him from shooting the wrong dog."

Western glanced sideways. "The wrong dog?" he repeated. He swung up to the right, heading for Dora Janeki's bleak farm.

"Tess," Mandy explained. "She's the stray Border collie we found. Dora took her in. But now she thinks Tess is the sheep worrier."

Western grimaced. "And you two say it's *my* dog, is that it?" He stopped.

Mandy's heart missed a beat. "We *saw* Major attacking the sheep, Mr. Western! It was Tess who tried to save them!"

"Hmmm." Sam Western seemed to be thinking of his warm fireside and slippers. He glanced back toward his house. "You could be trying to shift the blame here. I wouldn't put it past you."

"No, honestly!"

He sniffed. "Better not risk it, I suppose." Reluctantly he trudged on through the snow. "Isn't that Dora Janeki right over there?" He pointed to the hillside, where three tiny figures were coming down the slope toward them. He raised a hand and gave a loud shout.

While Sam Western rested and waited by a low wall, Mandy and James jumped over it and ran to meet the group. They recognized Whistler by his mottled gray coat and stooped to give him a welcoming pat. "Good boy," Mandy breathed. She looked up to see Dora, Dennis Saville, and another boy from Sam Western's farm approaching.

"It's the boss," the boy said to Dennis. He hung back to let the estate manager deal with what looked like trouble.

Dora came down frowning at Mandy. "We just spotted that stray dog and took a couple of shots at it. We haven't had any luck so far, but we will before the day's out!"

"But it's not Tess's fault," Mandy began. She felt James hold her back.

"Mandy, come over here!" He drew her away to listen to the conversation between Dennis Saville and Mr. Western.

"Where's the dog?" The farmer didn't bother with explanations. "Come on, Dennis, where's the darn thing gone?"

Dennis shuffled his feet. "Didn't he come back to the Hall?"

Western glowered but said nothing.

"He cut back home just after I brought him out. I saw him skirting back through the side gate. I figured he was headed straight home." Dennis Saville stood with his gun slung through the crook of his elbow. "Didn't he get there?"

"He did not." Sam Western sighed and took the phone from his pocket. "Let me call and check that he hasn't turned up there now." He pushed buttons to dial the number.

"What's all this about?" Dora demanded. "Whatever it is we'd better sort it out and get a move on. Have you seen those big, dark clouds? I don't like the look of them."

On the horizon, a bank of heavy snow clouds gathered. The sun had sunk behind them, leaving a golden rim of bright light.

Sam Western spoke into the phone. "What's that? No sign of Major, eh?" He listened. His frown deepened further. "Say that again!" he demanded.

Mandy and James held their breaths. They stamped their feet and looked worried. Sam Western seemed to have gone pale as he clicked a button and put the phone back in his pocket.

"Well?" Dora was anxious to press on.

"That was a message from my secretary," he said quietly. "She's just had a phone call from the Spillers' place. Word's going around that another sheep has been attacked about half an hour ago. Jack Spiller's on the scene right now. No one actually saw what happened, but the sheep's in a bad way. She's losing blood. They've just sent for the vet from Animal Ark. Spiller wants the dog caught before it does any more damage. Every farmer this side of Walton is out after it!"

"See!" Mandy cried. "You have to believe us! Major is a menace to every sheep around. Not Tess — Major!"

Her pleas fell on deaf ears.

"What's it matter which one it is?" Dora said. "We know there are two dogs on the loose up there. And there are more sheep being savaged. Let's go!" She marched across the hill, followed by Sam Western, Dennis Saville, and young Dean, Western's farmhand.

Mandy wanted to cry out in protest. Instead she turned to James. "Why won't they believe us?"

"Because they're not thinking straight, that's why. So *we'll* have to. Listen, Mandy, Mr. Western said that Jack Spiller called Animal Ark. Someone will be on his way right this minute. Let's run down to the road and try to head him off. That way we'll get to Spillers' first and explain about Major. There's a better chance that your mom or dad can make people believe what's happening than we can!"

Mandy agreed. Without another moment's hesitation, they sped off in the opposite direction to the gang with the guns, downhill toward the winding road, scanning the valley for a glimpse of the Animal Ark jeep.

"There!" Mandy cried. There was a gleam of windshield lower down the valley, the faint sound of an engine, before a blast of wind drowned it out and a flurry of snowflakes began to fall. They ran on toward the road.

When the jeep climbed into view again, Mandy and James stood in the midst of a sudden blizzard. They waved their arms and shouted. Dr. Adam skidded to a halt.

"Mandy! James!" He flung open the passenger door and told them to get in quickly.

"Are you going up to the Spillers'?" Mandy sank back against the seat, with James beside her.

Dr. Adam revved the engine. He turned the high beams on. "Yes, if we make it," he warned. "How did you know?"

Mandy explained in a rush how Mr. Western and his dog Major were suddenly involved; how it was Major who attacked Jack Spiller's sheep. "We have to stop the farmers from going after Tess!" she pleaded. "Can you tell them that she isn't to blame?"

Adam Hope frowned and nodded. "I'll do my best." The jeep edged forward up the slippery hill. "But remember, my most important job is to save Jack Spiller's sheep!"

Mandy nodded and hung on as the car skidded and bumped along.

At last they arrived at the small farm. Snow still fell thick and fast. Mrs. Spiller came out to the gate and di-

rected them off the road, along a rough track between
two stone walls, already hidden by snowdrifts. "You'll
have to drive about three hundred yards up the tractor
track!" she yelled. "Jack's stayed up there with the
sheep!"

They drove on. The car lurched and swayed. Soon
they spotted a dark figure bending over the injured
sheep. Dr. Adam stopped the car and ran across, knee-
deep in snow. Mandy and James ran to help.

Jack had covered the sheep with a piece of sacking to
keep off the worst of the snow. There was a wound low
down on its neck, and a stain of blood on the white
ground. Mandy winced as her father went down onto
his knees, opened up the bag she gave him, and injected
the shoulder with a shot of anesthetic. He waited for it
to take effect while he cleaned the wound. "It doesn't
look as if she's lost too much blood," he assured the
farmer. "And at least this one isn't pregnant."

Jack Spiller nodded. "Are you going to put in a couple
of stitches to stop the bleeding?"

Adam Hope worked fast. "That's what I'm doing now.
There. Now, Jack, you'll have to help me lift her into the
back of the jeep. That's right."

Mandy and James picked up the sacking and walked
behind her dad, Jack Spiller, and the sheep. She handed
her father his bag as he climbed up into his seat.

"Hop in the back with the patient," he told them.

But Jack interrupted. "There's more bad news, I'm afraid. Dennis Saville came down this way with a boy and a dog, just before you showed up. He asked me to tell you there's another one up the hill, not far off." His face looked drawn and worried as he pointed across the snow-swept hillside.

"Another injured sheep?" Dr. Adam roared the engine into life, grabbed his bag, and jumped to the ground again. "Has this dog gone crazy?" He pulled Jack Spiller toward the car. "Here, Jack; you'll have to drive your sheep down to the house in the jeep. Mandy and James, you stay with him. I'll have to go and take a look!"

Mandy began to protest as Jack Spiller climbed into the driver's seat.

"No, get the sheep down into the warmth as quickly as you can!" Dr. Adam ordered. He zipped his jacket to the chin, ready to set off across country.

"Dad!" Mandy said. "Wait for me. I want to come!"

But her dad insisted. "Stay in the car, Mandy. That's right. You'll have to help Jack at the other end. Carry the sheep inside with him. Keep her warm. Now go on, I won't be long!"

Mandy and James did as they were told. The snow gusted against the car, the wipers whined, the engine stuttered.

"Let's go," Jack Spiller said. "If we're not quick, the poor thing will die of cold!"

So Mandy and James clung to the bar as the jeep rattled back down to the cottage. The last Mandy saw of her father was a small, dim figure heading into the blizzard to save another life.

Eleven

The snow fell fast and furious. At Jack Spiller's house, Mandy and James helped carry the injured sheep into the small barn, where they settled her into a bed of straw and left Jenny and Maggie Spiller to take care of her.

"Sam Western's waiting in the house," Mrs. Spiller said. "He wants to have a word with you, Jack."

They went ahead and found the small kitchen swarming with people who had taken refuge from the sudden storm. Dora Janeki sat at the table with Dennis Saville and Dean. They huddled over cups of tea, guns resting against a nearby wall. Everyone avoided meeting

Mandy's and James's eyes as they came in. Dennis shuf-fled his feet in embarrassment.

Mr. Western himself stood by the window, clearing his throat. He took a step forward. "Er, Jack, I need to have a quiet word." He looked uncomfortable as he beckoned Jack across.

Mandy glanced at James. Mr. Western was not his usual confident self. She listened hard, trying to over-hear the conversation.

"Dennis saw it all . . . yes, the second sheep . . . he was there . . . I'm afraid it was . . . yes, Major, my new dog . . . most awfully sorry!" Sam Western mut-tered.

Mandy caught disjointed phrases. She held her breath as she saw Jack Spiller frown and nod. Then she couldn't bear to be in the dark any longer. She went up to Dennis Saville. "What happened?" she asked.

"Well, we caught Major in the act," he confessed, glancing at Dora's stern face. "We came along the ridge looking for the Border collie, and found Major attack-ing another of Jack's sheep. Dean here managed to grab him from behind, and we brought him straight down. We put him in the shed outside until the snow stops and we decide what to do with him."

Mandy's eyes filled up with relief. At last they knew

the truth. She turned to Dora. "Does that mean that you won't go after Tess anymore?"

Dora nodded. "I owe you and James an apology," she said gently. "I was a bit hasty. I'm sorry."

James came up with a smile. "What will happen to Major now?" He stood next to Mandy in a pool of melting snow.

"That depends." Dennis Saville kept one eye on his boss, still deep in conversation with Jack Spiller. "We want to hear what Jack has to say. After all, it's his sheep and Dora's here that have been attacked. I think Mr. Western still wants to keep him on and have him properly trained as a guard dog."

Mandy agreed that this was a good idea. "There's no need to have him put to sleep, is there?" Even though Major was the one who had caused all the trouble, she would never want to see a healthy animal put to death. "If he's treated well, I'm sure he'll improve!" She kept her fingers crossed for the poor dog, who didn't know how to use his freedom on the hillsides, after a life cooped up in a city yard.

At last Jack and Mr. Western came to an agreement. "I'll pay your vets' fees, and Mrs. Janeki's, too," Western announced. "I'll cover all the expenses that this trouble has caused. And I promise to keep Major well under control in the future. He's a fine animal, really, and I intend to look after him well."

Jack nodded. "If you stick to your promise and there's no more trouble from Major, I think we'd all agree with that."

Dora Janeki, too, came around. She sniffed and grumbled for a while, but in the end she didn't object. It ended in handshakes, relief, and smiles.

But outside the snow still fell. It whirled through the door in a great gust as Maggie Spiller and Jenny came in to report that the injured sheep was recovering well in the barn.

"Is Dad back yet?" Mandy asked. Through the window she could see the snow drifting up to three feet deep against the farmyard walls. It was more than half an hour since Adam Hope had set off after the second injured animal.

"No. I thought he might be in here," Mrs. Spiller looked anxiously around the room. "Shouldn't he be back by now?"

Mandy peered again through the window. She could hardly see beyond the tiny yard; the hillside was lost in the snowstorm. Dark clouds swept down, and the wind gusted. There was no sign at all of her brave father.

"Dennis, you know the spot where the sheep was." Mr. Western took charge. "How far is it from here?"

"About half a mile. I couldn't be sure, exactly. We were busy keeping Major under control." Dennis Saville looked at his watch. "Let's give him about ten more minutes before we start to worry."

They agreed. The minutes dragged by. Mandy sat with her face at the window staring out, praying for the snow to ease. And still Dr. Adam didn't show up.

"All right!" Mr. Western broke the edgy silence. "Let's make up a search party. We can't wait any longer. This is an emergency."

Mandy felt a jolt of fear pass through her. She watched the others put on their boots again and zip up their jackets. "Can I call my mom?" she asked Mrs. Spiller.

"Of course." She pointed to the phone.

Quickly Mandy went and dialed the number, urging her mother to hurry and pick up the phone. "Mom, it's me. I'm at the Spillers'. Dad's missing in the snow. We're sending out a search party." She spoke in a rush, then stopped short. There was a long pause. "Mom, are you there?"

"Yes, Mandy. I got all that. I'll run down to Grandpa at the village hall and get him to drive me straight up. Don't worry, we'll find him. Your dad knows what to do in these situations. We'll soon have him back safe and sound." Emily Hope hung up.

Mandy put down the phone. She felt less afraid. Her mom's calm voice was a huge help. Now she passed on the message to Mrs. Spiller. "Mom will try to get up here with Grandpa. Can you watch out for them, please?" She rushed to the door to follow Mr. Western's search party.

"Don't split up," he was telling the group as they emerged into the freezing white air. "Stick together. Dennis will have to lead the way. Come on!" Together they tramped out onto the tractor track, heads down, forming a tight bunch as they set off up the hill.

Mandy settled into the pace, steady but slow through the soft snow. She wore her scarf wrapped high around her face, but still the freezing wind tore through her and the snowflakes blinded her. Beside her, James struggled to lift his legs clear of the snow with each wearying step.

Up ahead, Dennis came to a halt. "I think it's this way now." They cut off to the left like Arctic explorers, into a wilderness that no one recognized.

For a few more minutes they trekked over the uneven ground. Mandy stepped into a snow-covered hollow up to her waist.

James hauled her out. "We must be nearly there!" he gasped.

But Dennis had hesitated a second time. "I was sure it was this way!" He searched all around for landmarks, but covered in snow, the terrain was strange and unfamiliar. The group scanned the hillside without seeing any sign of Adam Hope and the sheep.

"Try shouting!" Sam Western suggested.

The call went up in every direction. They cupped gloved hands to their mouths and shouted for the vet. But the snow deadened their cries, and there was no reply.

Dennis Saville shook his head. He turned to Dean. "Which way now?"

"It all looks different. I couldn't say."

"And how long has he been out in this now?" Dora Janeki asked. She looked grim, as if she knew there was a limit to what a person lost in the snow could stand.

"About an hour and a half," Jack Spiller said.

Mandy scoured the snowy slopes for signs of her father — footsteps, a half-covered trail. But the snow drifted as it landed, and wiped away all tracks. She felt a hopelessness settle on them. "Dad!" she called out. The hillside threw back a dead, muffled silence. She looked desperately at James.

"Well, this is no good. I suggest we go back to the house," Sam Western decided. "We've gone wrong somehow. It's no one's fault. Conditions up here are terrible. We'd better get on the phone to the rescue service and get them up here as fast as we can."

He turned and led them down the hill, using his mobile phone to call for paramedics and the police. They had to guess their way back to Jack Spiller's place, arriving weary and downhearted as Mrs. Spiller threw open the door to greet them.

"We can't find him!" Mandy ran the last few yards and dashed into the kitchen. "Is Mom here yet?"

"No. No one's gotten through so far." Mrs. Spiller had hot tea waiting.

Jack told his wife that the police were sending a rescue vehicle from Walton. The police realized it was an emergency — a man missing on the hill in this weather. They would pull out all the stops.

But the waiting was dreadful for Mandy. She stood with James out on the porch, straining to hear the sound of a car engine, longing for her mom to arrive. She looked for headlights in the snow, imagining them and then feeling her hopes die. At last she caught a sound and struggled out into the snow, across the yard to the gate. Sure enough, her grandfather's camper came crawling up the hill, skidding sideways, its back wheels sliding and kicking up snow.

Mandy ran down the hill. Her mom jumped out of the van, dressed in a heavy blue jacket and boots. Grandpa braked into the side of the road and turned off the lights. He ran to join them.

"Oh, Mom, hurry!" Mandy cried. "We can't find him. The snow's too bad. He's lost!"

Emily Hope nodded. "Okay, keep calm. Which way?" She turned to her father-in-law. "Let's take another look."

"This way! We went up with the first search party, but we all got lost." She waded into a drift, toward the two stone walls that showed the line of the tractor track. They were still just visible under the snow. She wondered how her mom could stay so calm.

They all set their faces against a head wind and struggled on. "Here!" James came to the end of the tractor track. "This is where we found the first sheep, remember!" This time he felt they were on the right track. "And Dr. Adam headed up that way to the second sheep!"

Mandy nodded. She felt a flicker of hope. But as they sank waist-deep into more drifts, she grew desperate again. She heard Grandpa begin to shout out his son's name. Snow whirled down without end. Still they pressed on.

Then Mandy stopped. She thought she heard a low whine. She told herself that it was impossible, but she peered through the storm. "Wait a minute, Grandpa! Did you hear that?"

There was another whine, coming nearer, and a bark.

"Tess!" Mandy would have recognized the sound anywhere. "Here, girl!" They stood fixed to the spot, waiting for her to appear.

A shape scrambled down the hill. It was Tess. Her dark coat was matted with frozen snow, but her brown eyes were alert, her tail carried high. She bounded toward Mandy, who fell to the ground to hug her.

Grandpa, James, and Emily Hope came crowding around. "Good girl!" James told her. "At least we can take you back with us this time!" He told Dr. Emily the story of who had really attacked the sheep.

"Hold on a minute; it looks like she wants us to follow, not the other way around!" Grandpa pulled Mandy to her feet and stood looking at Tess. The dog barked and ran up the hill a little way. Then she came back and barked again. She looked up at Mandy, darted away, and came back.

"She does!" Mandy could see she wanted to show them something.

Right away they set off after Tess, treading deep into new snow, only waiting when Tess stopped to listen, ears pricked up. Then she dashed forward again, impatient for them to follow.

"Is she up to what I think she's up to?" Grandpa asked. "Is she trying to show us where Adam is?"

Mandy looked at her mom and grandfather and nodded. "I'm sure that's what she's doing!" She plowed ahead, with James at her side.

"What do you think?" Mandy's grandfather asked Emily Hope.

"I think we should trust her."

Mandy heard them hurry to catch up. "Go on, Tess! Show us the way. Good girl!" Still the dog struggled shoulder-deep through the snow, looking, listening. She answered a signal with a sharp bark and a swift change of direction.

"What was that? I didn't hear anything!" James said.

"No, but Tess did. Come on!" Mandy would have trusted her to the ends of the earth.

At last, after what seemed like forever, Tess came to a steep dip. It ran twenty yards to a row of beech trees beside a frozen stream. Tess waited for them, then bounded down the slope.

"Listen!" Mandy said. "I heard a whistle!"

James nodded. They ran after Tess, half-tumbling, skidding and sliding down the hill. "Where, Tess? Where is he? Show us, girl!"

Snow had drifted against the trees in white mounds that came shoulder-high. Tess was light, able to leap from mound to mound. The whistle grew louder.

"Dad!" Mandy called. She strained to see through the snowflakes. "Dad, where are you?"

There was a faint sound. "Here!"

Mandy shouted back. "Oh, Dad, thank heavens!" She turned to her mom and grandfather. "He's alive!" They came running down the hill. "Hang on, Dad! Tess is trying to find you. Whistle again!" She watched as Tess began to scrape with her front paws at the side of the farthest drift.

"Here!" Mandy heard her dad's muffled voice again. She and James scrambled to the far side of the drift and dropped onto their knees. They saw a deep tunnel scooped into the snow. Mandy leaned inside. She found the huddled shape of their father waiting patiently for rescue.

Tess bounded up the slope and barked out their success. The others came running. Emily Hope fell to the ground and wriggled into the snow hole to check Adam's condition. There were tears in her eyes as she crawled back out. "Let's lift him out," she said. "I think he's going to be all right, but we'll have to go carefully."

Gently they lifted Mandy's father out of the shelter he'd dug into the snow. He was stiff and numb. Snow had frozen into his beard, he couldn't feel his feet, and his legs could scarcely stand.

"Don't forget the sheep," he told them. "Try and pull her out as well."

Grandpa and James dug deep into the tunnel. They scraped the snow out until they found the animal. She was still alive.

"We'll have to carry her down to Jack's place," Adam Hope insisted. He staggered and tried to stand.

"*You* won't be carrying anyone," Emily Hope told him. She watched as Mandy helped to steady him and slung his arm around her shoulder. "You'll have enough trouble carrying yourself down. Here, let me help."

Mandy looked up at her dad, tears in her eyes. "Can you walk?" she whispered.

He nodded and found his balance.

"We'll bring the sheep," James said. He and Mandy's grandfather began to work out how they should carry her. Emily Hope took her husband's hand and began to lead him up the slope.

Mandy stayed behind for a moment with Tess, by the snow hole that had stopped her father from freezing to death. "You saved his life," she whispered in the dog's soft ear. She tried to wipe the snow from Tess's back. "You're a wonderful dog, and now everyone knows it!" She spoke gently. "There's no danger now, Tess. You can come back with us." She got to her feet and walked a couple of paces up the hill. "Come on, girl!"

But Tess had completed her task. She'd saved Adam Hope's life. Now she turned away from Mandy and began to tread lightly up the opposite slope.

"Tess, here, girl!"

The dog didn't falter. She walked on, up the hill toward High Cross, without looking back.

Mandy watched her go. How could Tess know that it was safe to come back? She wished she could make her understand. She wished dogs knew human words. She longed to take her home.

But Mandy watched in silence as Tess reached the top of the ridge. The clouds lifted now; the snow began to clear. Mandy could follow Tess's lonely shape along the white horizon. She didn't call again.

With a sad heart she turned to follow her father, her mother, Grandpa, and James. The dog who'd saved many lives was a stray again. She was homeless on Christmas Eve, wandering the snowy hills.

Twelve

"Tess certainly saved us a hard job!" the paramedic told Mandy. They'd arrived just in time to see Adam Hope being brought off the hillside by members of his own family. All the rescue team needed to do was to check that he wouldn't suffer any long-term effects from his afternoon in the snow. "That dog of yours must be some kind of heroine!"

Mandy had told him all about Tess, how her sharp hearing had picked up Dr. Adam's whistle, how she'd come to find them and show them the way. She stood by as the rescue team led her dad into the ambulance and insisted on seeing him safely home.

Sam Western and his group of rescuers stood at the Spillers' gate, watching them go. All had ended well. Both sheep would recover, thanks to Adam Hope. And Mr. Western had taken the blame squarely on his own shoulders.

Dora Janeki came forward to tell Mandy how she felt: "I'd take Tess back right now if I could." They watched Emily Hope climb up into the ambulance and the doors close. "We'd have to go a long way to find another dog like that!"

Mandy nodded. But she said nothing. The truth had come out too late to save Tess.

"I really am sorry." Dora patted Mandy's shoulder and walked away.

"Come on, you two!" Grandpa came and told James and Mandy to jump into the camper. "Let's follow the ambulance. We can go and tell your grandmother that everyone's safe."

So they left the hillside, still deep in snow. The storm had died as quickly as it had come, and the skies were clear. The afternoon was ending in pale sunlight that sparkled along the hilltop.

They went home to Welford. Mrs. Hunter met James in the village and took him back to their house. Grandma stood waiting anxiously outside the village hall. She watched the ambulance drive past with Adam and Emily safe inside. Grandpa stopped the van for her to climb in. "Don't worry, everyone's fine!" he told her.

Grandma took a deep breath. "Of course everyone's fine!" she said. "I warned you not to make a fuss. Adam knows what he's doing." She turned to smile at Mandy. "We Hopes are a tough lot!"

Mandy was secretly glad that Grandma hadn't been out in that blizzard. No matter how tough the Hopes were, she knew her dad wouldn't have survived much longer.

"And . . ." Grandma announced proudly as they followed the ambulance up the driveway to Animal Ark ". . . everything's ready for the party! We went ahead and brought the food over to the hall. It's all set out, ready and waiting!"

"Grandma, are you sure?" Mandy slid open the side door and jumped down into a foot and a half of crunchy snow. "I thought we might have to cancel it after all this!"

Grandma stepped down and stood, hands on hips. "Cancel! Just because of a little snowstorm?" She made it sound like a ridiculous idea. "Whoever heard of a drop of snow stopping us from enjoying ourselves at Christmas?"

Slowly Mandy's face broke into a smile. She went up and hugged her grandmother, letting a quiet tear fall for Tess, who wouldn't be there to join in the fun.

"There, that's better," Grandma said gently. "Now dry your eyes and get yourself into the party spirit. In spite of everything, I have a feeling that this is going to be the best Christmas Eve you can ever remember!"

The snowplows drove out from Walton to clear the main roads. Farmers brought out their tractors and cleared a way through from the high farms down to the village. Snow lay heaped against the walls in white banks that dwarfed the cars as they came down to the village for the candlelit gathering at the Fox and Goose.

Mandy arrived just before half past seven. Mrs. Ponsonby was already there with Pandora and Toby. Pandora was decked out in a Christmas ribbon tied around her neck in an enormous bow. John Hardy came out with Button and Barney warmly snuggled inside a spare cat carrier. He wore a pirate's hat and an eye patch, to the amusement of little Claire McKay, who had just turned up with James's Blackie. She wore a cardboard crown covered in gold foil, with rubies and diamonds made of shiny hard candies stuck on around the rim. Everyone laughed and chattered. Grandma arrived with a tray of candles stuck into oranges, decorated with spices, candies, and red ribbon. She began to light them and hand them around. The party was about to begin.

Mandy took a peek insider her jacket at Mopsy, the favorite of her three pet rabbits, curled up safe and warm inside a specially made sling. Her ears twitched. Her sleepy eyes blinked back at Mandy.

"Hi, Brandon!" Claire and Blackie ran to meet the latest arrivals. Mrs. Gill had dropped Brandon and Ruby the pig in the pub parking lot. Ruby was wearing the party hat, a battered straw number decorated with plastic sunflowers. Brandon picked her up as she made a beeline for Pandora's shiny bow. "Behave yourself," he warned, red with embarrassment.

Mandy knew that Grandpa had driven the van up onto the hill again to fetch Lydia and Houdini. He brought them now, with young Jenny Spiller and her sheep. The door opened and they tumbled out into the snowy yard, noisy and excited. Houdini kicked up his heels, ready to make a break. "Steady, boy!" Lydia warned. She held him back. "I guess he's looking for something to eat," she explained.

Soon Walter Pickard came out of the pub with old Tom, his chewed ear ragged but nicely healed. Ernie Bell followed with Sammy, proudly producing his cap from his pocket and pinning a sprig of mistletoe to the side. He put it on his gray, stubbly head. "You never know your luck!" he grinned. He and Lydia got ready to join the procession together.

"Where's James?" Mandy looked around the glowing group. She took a candle from her grandma. "He should be here by now."

Grandma looked mysterious. "I expect Eric is acting up. Maybe James has had to stop and look for him."

"Oh, but hadn't we better wait for them?" Mandy didn't want to start without James.

"We could go ahead," Grandma said. "I'm sure he wouldn't mind!"

Mandy frowned. It wasn't like James to be late for something so important.

Next Andi Greenaway turned up from Manor Farm. She led Dorian along the main street. The old donkey stepped sturdily through the snow, his large, flat feet plodding softly, his nose poking over all the garden gates as he came along. Andi was dressed in an old striped blanket, with a dish towel tied around her head, carrying a shepherd's crook in her hand. "I'm a Christmas shepherd," she told Brandon and John. "Anyone can see that!"

But the star was Susan Collins with Prince. She arrived five minutes later, riding tall in a red sombrero. Her wide brim was laden with fake oranges, bananas, pineapples, and grapes. Prince wore one to match, with holes cut in the crown for his ears, the brim tilted at a jaunty angle. Susan wore a Spanish guitar slung across her shoulder, and a silvery shirt covered in frills and ruffles.

"Oh, my!" Mrs. Ponsonby cried, as Pandora ran yapping toward the late arrivals.

Dorian and Ruby wandered across to investigate the fruit. The little pig snorted and snuffled. Dorian backed off, disappointed to find that the pineapples were plastic. Susan laughed. "Sorry I'm late!" she called.

"Ready?" Mrs. Ponsonby scooped Pandora into her arms and called Toby to her. She formed them into a procession and struck up the first carol.

> *Good King Wenceslas looked out*
> *On the Feast of Stephen . . .*

She stood at the head of the line, hitting a lively rhythm. Soon the others joined in.

"Don't worry about James," Grandma winked at Mandy. "He'll soon catch up!"

The procession was on the move. Mandy stood holding her candle, waiting until the last minute. She gazed down the road for any sign of her best friend.

"Come on, Mandy!" Mrs. Ponsonby urged from up front.

So Mandy joined them, breaking into song.

> *. . . Brightly shone the moon that night,*
> *Though the frost was cruel,*
> *When a poor man came in sight,*
> *Gathering winter fu-u-el!*

It was a lovely sight, the long, candlelit procession trailing down the snow-covered street. The sound of music rang out; the stars shone down from a clear sky. People came to their doors to smile and join in the Christmas spirit. The guests slowly made their way, pets and owners, all shapes and sizes, ages, colors; all part of the magical event.

Mrs. Ponsonby drew them to a halt outside the porch of the village hall. Everyone stood around in a semicircle to finish their song.

"Come on, Mandy," Grandma whispered, taking her by the arm and leading her forward.

"What's going on?" Mandy found herself surrounded by smiling faces lit by soft yellow candlelight. She was gently drawn to the front. Sammy the squirrel darted onto her shoulder and ran chattering up and down

her arm. Then he sat perched, his tail brushing her cheek.

"Go ahead." Mrs. Ponsonby stepped aside with a gracious gesture. "This is *your* party, Mandy. Without you, none of this would have happened!"

Many took a deep, deep breath. She delved inside her jacket to take Mopsy out of the sling she'd made to cradle him. Sammy still sat jauntily on her shoulder. She handed her candle to Ernie and kicked the snow off her boots. Then she stepped onto the porch and opened the door.

Inside the brilliantly lit hall, her mom and dad stood waiting to greet her. Mom's red hair was swept onto the top of her head. She wore her best blue party dress and smiled happily. Dad, showered and spruced up, and none the worse for his ordeal, stood with his arm around his wife's waist.

Beyond them, all Mandy could see through her happy tears was a riot of colored balloons, streamers, holly, Christmas lights, and the tall green tree. She smelled spicy fruit punch, heard festive music drifting from the loudspeakers. The lights seemed to float and swim. The whole room was alive.

Then she saw James walking toward her, carrying Eric. She felt the other guests jostle her forward. She heard Grandma whisper in her ear. "Look, Mandy. Look who James has brought!"

James grinned as he gave a command. "Sit, girl! Tess, sit!"

Mandy stared down at his feet.

Tess sat looking back at her with her liquid brown eyes. Someone had brushed her coat to a smooth, glossy shine. Her white chest and the white stripe down her muzzle gleamed. At the sight of Mandy, her tail swept the floor, back and forth.

"Tess!" Mandy felt Sammy jump from her shoulder in surprise. She handed Mopsy to her grandmother. Then she went forward to touch the dog, to make it real, so that she wouldn't wake up and find this all a dream. She ran her hand down Tess's neck and patted her shoulder. "Is it really you?" she breathed.

Tess growled softly. Then Ruby came in and broke them apart with her little hard hooves and soft snout. She buffeted Tess out of the way, heading straight for the nearest food.

"Where . . . ? How . . . ? When?" The questions tumbled out as the party began.

James explained everything. He'd persuaded his mother to take him back up to High Cross before it got dark. Ken Hudson had spotted him and agreed to help find Tess. They knew which way she'd headed after the rescue. They had found Tess's trail by the Celtic cross and began to call her name. Lydia came out of her house and said she'd seen a dog in the woods at the back of the farm. James and Ken ran to find her curled up in an exhausted sleep in the shelter of a tumbledown wall. Ken had put her on a leash and they took her back to Dora's, who soon set her right with food and good care. Ken had brought Tess down to the village in time for James to bring her to the party in secret.

"I wanted it to be a surprise for you!" he said.

"It was!" Mandy felt her heart swell. "It's perfect! It's everything I ever wished! Thank you, James. Oh, thank you!"

"So Tess is the guest of honor?" Grandpa stepped carefully between cats and dogs to come and speak to them. "I'm glad everything's worked out fine."

Mandy smiled. She sat with Tess at her feet as Mrs. Ponsonby organized the competition. She awarded the party-hat prize to Prince and Susan just before Houdini snatched a bite at the pony's felt sombrero. Then Simon played more music, the pets got their party food, and the people were fed, too. Grandma brought hot mince pies from the small kitchen, and Pandora disgraced herself over the pigs in blankets.

All in all, the party was a great success. Everyone agreed that the pets behaved perfectly — even Mrs. Ponsonby said so!

"Of course!" Mandy said to James. She still sat with one arm around Tess's neck.

He smiled at her. She smiled back. They'd made it. Everyone was safe, Tess had a home, the pets were at their party. "Merry Christmas, James!" she said. "A very, very merry Christmas!"